CLOSE UP NOW, WITH ONLY THE BED BETWEEN THEM, Koko looked all muscle and sharp claw, covered by thick gray hide, too big, too hungry. It was death on four legs, more terrifying than bursting into flames or being bitten by a rattler or poisoned by touching rabbit food, or even being raped and cut up. It was more horrid than anything her OCD ever could have conjured.

And it was coming toward her.

WICKED DEAD

PREY

BY
STEFAN PETRUCHA
AND THOMAS PENDLETON

HARPER TEEN

AN IMPRINT OF HARPERCOLLINSPUBLISHERS

Grateful acknowledgment is given to Shaun O'Boyle
for the use of the title page image, © Shaun O'Boyle.
More of his evocative photographs can be seen on
www.oboylephoto.com.

HarperTeen is an imprint of
HarperCollins Publishers.

Wicked Dead: Prey

www.harperteen.com

Library of Congress Cataloging-in-Publication Data
Petrucha, Stefan.
   Prey / by Stefan Petrucha and Thomas Pendleton.—1st ed.
      p. cm.—(Wicked dead)
   Summary: Sixteen-year-old Chelsea's obsessive-compulsive dis-
order (OCD) causes her to believe she must continually count
objects to prevent awful things from happening, but when she
agrees to pet-sit her biology teacher's six-foot monitor lizard,
counting may not be enough.
   ISBN 978-0-06-113853-9 (pbk.)
   [1. Obsessive-compulsive disorder—Fiction. 2. Monitor
lizards—Fiction. 3. Pet sitting—Fiction. 4. Counting—Fiction. 5.
Horror stories.] I. Pendleton, Thomas, DATE– II. Title.
PZ7.P44727Pre 2008   2007009131
[Fic]—dc22   CIP
                                                              AC

Typography by Christopher Stengel

First Edition

THOMAS PENDLETON DEDICATES THIS
BOOK TO QUENTIN SHOCK KLEIN, ONE
OF THE NEW BLOOD.

STEFAN PETRUCHA DEDICATES THIS
BOOK TO MAIA, WHO KNOWS IT
MUCH BETTER THAN HE.

PROLOGUE

This place knew fear.

Over the years, thousands of children had spent time in Lockwood Orphanage. Infants and toddlers, children, and young adults lived between its walls, and fright was a familiar companion, whether it was a little boy's terror of the bogeyman beneath his bed or an older girl's dread of an English teacher's lewd stares. Fear of the dark. Fear of punishment. Fear of being alone. Fear of the teachers and the staff and the strangers who came to look at them like pigs at a fair. All of these terrors, and many more, belonged to the orphans of Lockwood.

The children were all gone now. Some were adopted. Others grew up and moved on. And still others died within the structure that had been built to protect them. The fear remained, though. It thrived in the walls and the floors like mold. It clung to the light fixtures and the doorjambs like dust. You couldn't take a step in the decrepit old building without it getting on you, a filthy reminder of what had happened there. At one time or another, every living thing that entered this edifice felt fear.

But it was best known to those trapped in this place.

No. No. No, Shirley's panicked mind screamed. *Nonononono!*

Everything around her was a frantic blur. The walls flew by like a racing fog bank. Doorways appeared as nothing more than black smudges in the rushing haze. Daphne's face rose before her—eyes wild, her mouth covered by a smoky black ribbon—only to vanish a second later. Yanked and jostled and bound tightly within the Headmistress's vicious grip, Shirley felt certain she would lose her mind.

Mary appeared, suspended high above the hallway by another murky tentacle, her blonde ringlets whipping crazily in the air. She sailed too high and the top of her head disappeared into the ceiling. The Headmistress sent Mary higher, making it look like her head was gone and her shoulders dragged across the chipped and stained plaster above. A chandelier passed through Mary's chest and back like a wrecking ball.

The Headmistress charged ahead of them all, her form misty black, like squid ink discharged in a raging tidal current.

Shirley cried out against the band covering her mouth. It reeked of char and rot, and it scalded her lips and tongue.

Even more dreadful than her capture was the knowledge of where she was being taken. The Red Room! That was the Headmistress's place of punishment. Her chamber of pain. Though Shirley had spent no time within its damned walls, she'd seen what a night in the Red Room had done to the others. She'd seen the horror playing in her friends' eyes, etched into their irises like nightmare tattoos.

She couldn't go there. It would kill her.

But you're already dead.

Then it would be worse than death; it would be a visit to hell. And she knew the girl who'd bought her ticket.

Why, Anne? Why? We gave you three turns. What else could we do?

Her headlong rush down the hallway began to slow, and her panic intensified. She could already see

3

the door to the Red Room, looming ahead as frightening as a guillotine. The smoky form of the Headmistress went rigid. Shirley felt herself flying forward as if being thrown at the wall.

Then she came to a jerking stop. Disoriented, she stumbled back and threw her hands out to keep from falling. Her back touched the door of the Red Room and she yelped in horror.

She stood between Daphne and Mary. They too were trying to stabilize themselves. Mary teetered to the side and dropped to a knee. Daphne bent at the waist, gripping her knees tightly, her hair falling forward like a valance to cover her face. Before them stood the Headmistress, no longer a dark cloud, but in her human form. She patted the bun of hair on her head and then punched her fists onto the curves of her hips. She lifted her chin, revealing the tight white collar of her blouse and the narrow neck it strangled.

"Deceitful brats," she hissed. "Do you really think you can just leave this place?"

"We weren't trying to leave," Daphne said quickly.

"That's right," Shirley blurted out. "Anne's just angry with us because . . ."

"Shirley," Mary warned, "you're excited. Maybe you shouldn't talk just now."

4

Oh no, Shirley thought. Mary was right. She'd almost spilled her guts about the bones. She clamped her teeth on her thumbnail and gnawed through a thick edge. With her other hand she twirled a lock of hair, screwing it tightly around her finger until it felt like it might tear from her scalp. She needed to stay quiet. Daphne would get them out of this, or Mary. They were smart. They knew how to talk when things got bad.

She ripped away the bit of thumbnail. A sharp pain flared along her hand and then vanished. She looked at the wounded digit. The nail had already grown back. She put it in her mouth and started chewing all over again.

"Anne is upset with us," Daphne continued. "I don't know what she told you, but we know we can't leave. There's nothing beyond these walls for us."

The Headmistress's eyes burned as she looked at each girl in turn. Her arms—bent and planted on her hips—were so tense they trembled.

"We've all tried to experience the world beyond the threshold," Mary said. "Not one of us has found anything but murk and fury and raging wind. It is a maelstrom. A symphony of damage, playing without intermission or end."

"Such pretty words," the Headmistress spat.

"Always so poetic, dear Mary. Do you find comfort in such immature blathering? Do the romantic phrases bring you *peace*?"

"They're all I have," Mary whispered cautiously, unsure how her response would be greeted. "Like the convict and his canary."

"Feh." The Headmistress lifted her chin a notch higher. "You've disobeyed me . . . again! The lot of you. Your black-haired friend tells me this has been going on for quite some time. Your plotting and deceiving, mocking all that I've tried to maintain."

"It's not true," Daphne said.

"It's not!" Shirley added, another wedge of fingernail flying from her lips. "It's not. Please. You have to believe us. It's Anne. She just . . ."

"Enough," the Headmistress shouted. "That's quite enough." She lowered her voice to a rumbling growl. "Your lies are like needles in my ears."

Behind her, Shirley felt the door to the Red Room shake. Her heart trembled with it, beating a rapid rhythm behind her ribs. Her thoughts collided and tangled. *This can't be happening. It can't. No. No. No. Please, no.*

"Some children only understand punishment," said the Headmistress.

6

The door to the Red Room flew open. Shirley felt it tear away from her, heard it slam against the wall.

Her fragile thoughts shattered. Desperate to be away from this horrible woman and her frightening retribution, she cried out, and broke to the right. She'd run and run. She'd hide with the rats in the kitchen or the basement. She'd never speak another word so the Headmistress would never find her.

Before she made it four steps, a bony arm wrapped around her chest. Fingers dug into her armpit. Shirley's feet left the ground as the Headmistress lifted her and pulled her close. She screamed and kicked, but the grip was too strong.

"Again, you disobey me," the Headmistress said. "Let's see how long your defiance lasts in here." She tossed Shirley over the threshold into the Red Room.

A moment later Daphne was beside her, and then Mary, both thrown like dolls into the room.

As the name suggested, the cracked walls of the Red Room were crimson, and so were the floor and ceiling. The surfaces oozed and pulsed as if they formed the chamber of a cold, sick heart. Except for the girls, it was empty. Wholly empty. No furniture occupied the floor and no paintings adorned the walls. But this emptiness was temporary. Fiendish things lived here, hid in the pulsing walls.

Shirley was frantic. She tore at her hair. She stomped in tight circles, sobbing, performing an anxious dance. Hands fell on her shoulders and she screamed, shaking them away, fearing they were the first terrors offered up by the Red Room.

"Have a splendid evening," the Headmistress called.

The door of the room slammed shut.

"Settle down, kid," Daphne said, trying to console Shirley. "You aren't doing yourself or us any good."

Shirley couldn't calm down, though. Her stomach was aching with worry and her thoughts, miserable images of what might emerge from this place, came too fast.

"We have to keep our heads," Daphne continued. "Maybe together it won't be so bad."

"B-but what if it is?" Shirley cried.

"We'll hold hands," Mary suggested. "We'll grasp one another tightly and face the coming dread. Through unity, each of us will have the strength of three."

"Great idea," Daphne said. She wiped her hands on the thighs of her striped pajamas and threw her arms out, offering her palms to the other girls. "We've always been alone before. Now we have each other. I'll bet we knock this thing down a peg or two tonight."

"What's going to happen?" Shirley whined, reaching out to take Daphne's hand, then Mary's.

"I don't remember," Daphne told her. "Once you leave this place the specifics go away. You just remember how it felt."

"How does it feel?" Shirley asked.

"Let's play a game," Mary chirped, obviously trying to change the subject. "Like when we were little girls. Something fun and whimsical."

"I don't remember any games," Shirley said. "Only the bone game, and we can't play that . . . because of Anne."

"We'll deal with her when we get out of here," Daphne said. Her face tightened with anger.

A noise, like the snapping of a twig, cracked at the back of the room. Shirley yelped. She turned her head toward the sound, but only saw the pulsing red walls.

"All of her talk of rats and living like animals." Mary shook her head. "She's a beast. Who knows what she's doing this very minute?"

"She's playing the game," Daphne said, clearly unhappy about it. "She's doing to us what we did to her."

"But we didn't tell on her," Shirley wept. "We

didn't trick her. It's not like we meant for the Headmistress to take her."

"I'm not saying it's the same thing," Daphne replied. "Anne just thinks it is. She's so afraid and angry, she can't see we're on the same side."

"I, for one, am *not* on her side. After this night, I intend to have nothing more to do with her. I would hope you two feel the same. . . ."

A second cracking interrupted Mary. This time it was louder, closer.

"It's beginning," Daphne said. Her usually strong voice sounded small and weak.

Shirley shuddered all over. She gripped the other girls' hands as tightly as she could, throwing glances over her shoulders to see what the Red Room produced. She knew that if she'd eaten she would throw up all over the floor. But she hadn't eaten in decades, so she was spared this humiliation. The urge to chew her nails was almost impossibly strong, but she refused to let go of the supportive hands. Shirley looked over her shoulder to the back of the room, thinking she would go completely mad if it weren't for the presence of her friends.

She turned back to the girls and screamed.

Daphne and Mary were gone. In their place stood

two monstrous corpses. The one on the left, where Daphne had been standing, had dead, white eyes. Its mouth twisted open in a silent scream. Spit foamed at the corners and dripped down its chin. Its body was bent and damaged, with deep cuts on the neck and arms. Next to this horrible visage stood the second corpse. Skin slid down its cheeks, revealing bright red meat beneath. Its jaw was unhinged and a fat purple tongue lolled like that of a panting dog.

Cries of terror peeled from Shirley's throat. She yanked and struggled, freeing her hands from the rotting dead. Stumbling back, she pivoted on her foot and fled to the back of the room. Suddenly, a red fog, like misty arterial spray, fell over her in a hot shower.

"Help!" she screamed, pawing her way through the scarlet haze. "Please help me."

A moment later the fog cleared, but what it revealed was far worse. Shirley stood in the center of a thousand reanimated corpses. They writhed under her feet and pressed in at her from all sides. Their gory hands reached for her, touching her hair and her neck, scratching her face with ragged yellowing nails. She pushed against them, trying to free herself. Seeing a small opening between two of the dead, she wedged her shoulder into the gap and pushed through. She tried to run but the crush of bodies was too great. She stumbled and nearly fell into the back of a girl wearing a pink flannel nightgown. The girl faced the other direction. What remained of her hair was tangled in the fingers of a tall, skeletal man.

The girl turned, and her image froze Shirley inside and out.

Shirley was looking at herself.

Her face was puffy and purple around the eyes. Her mouth drooped at the edges as if she'd died frowning. The dead girl lifted her hand to her mouth and slid her thumb between her teeth as if preparing to gnaw at the fingernail. Without blinking she chomped down, taking half of the digit off. She spat the meat out onto the backs of the squirming dead.

"Help me," Shirley's corpse whispered, lifting her hand toward her ghostly self.

Nothing could have been more awful. Shirley screamed and screamed until the wall of bodies closed in front of her, and she was again embraced on all sides by death.

Across the room Daphne and Mary endured their own private terrors. Mary crouched on the floor, sobbing. Daphne stood in the corner, absolutely rigid, but shaking all over.

And outside the room, past the Headmistress who guarded the door, along the hall and two floors below, Anne sat cross-legged on the floor of the infirmary. Next to her a great hole in the floor gaped. It opened to the basement below. Ragged boards formed a rough circle only inches from where Anne sat between two of the dusty cots with their fraying sheets. She cursed and gathered up the bones again.

35, she thought. She'd rolled the bones thirty-five times, and nothing. She shook the bones in a cupped hand and rolled them again.

36.

Damn it, Anne thought. The other girls probably put some kind of curse on the bones so that Anne couldn't use them. That would be exactly like those bitches. She hoped the Red Room was particularly nasty tonight. Maybe one of them—hopefully, *all* of them—would never come out. They deserved to suffer for the way they'd treated her.

"Come on," she told the bones.

She rolled again. *37.*

Just like heaven.

Numbers began to crowd into her head. Anne tried

to shake them away as she looked at the bones. Only one number concerned her. She needed three of the symbols. *3*.

And there they were.

Food pellets sifted lazily through Chelsea Kaüer's hand. One or two at a time, the rough green-brown nuggets tumbled across her fingers, down into the bowl. As they hit the plastic, she counted them in her head: *38, 39, 40, 41.*

She was being watched. She knew it. Four sets of hungry pink eyes followed her every move. Furry noses pressed against the tank's glass. White whiskers swished across the smooth transparent surface. She pretended not to notice.

63, 64, 65, 66.

Like the pellets in her hand, the pet store rabbits jostled each other, trying to push their way through the glass to reach the food that slowly filled the bowl.

72, 73, 74, 75.

A young voice intruded.

"Excuse me." It was said as if one word: *skewsmee.*

Already uncomfortable in her blue-and-red, one-size-too-small Rhett's Pets vest, Chelsea almost lost count.

Just a customer, she told herself, but still she closed her eyes a second and repeated, *75. 75. 75.*

Or else the food would turn to poison.

Pivoting on her knees toward the source of the voice, she found herself at eye level with a mop of brown curls and pink buttons in the shape of flowers down the center of an adorable purple dress. Toddler cuteness had yet to fade from the small intruder's face, so maybe she was four? Chelsea counted the years—*1, 2, 3, 4*—to keep the little girl from bursting into flames.

"I want to pet a puppy," she said. The standard request.

"Oh. Okay. Do you have a parent here?"

The girl jutted a small, sticky finger toward a dowdy woman near the store entrance, where puppies behind Plexiglas yipped and pranced. Loaded down with shopping bags, she seemed singularly unenchanted. Pete, the shift manager, was in the back room taking inventory, and Holly hadn't shown yet. It was up to Chelsea.

She gave the girl her best Disneyland grin.

"Be there in a minute, okay? I have to finish feeding the rabbits."

The girl nodded but didn't, as Chelsea had hoped, leave. Chelsea took another handful of food and counted faster, hoping the girl wouldn't notice or question.

138, 139, 140, 141.

She did both.

"Why are you counting? Why don't you just pour it out?"

141. 141. 141.

Chelsea kept the grin plastered on her face but lowered her voice. "I have something called OCD." Before the girl could ask, she added, "It's a kind of sickness in the brain. Sometimes when I'm nervous or tired, it makes me count."

"Are you nervous or tired?"

"Tired."

The cute little brow furrowed. "I count sometimes. It's not a sickness. How does it work?"

"Well, there's a part of my brain that says if I don't count, something very bad will happen."

177, 178, 179, 180.

"Like what?"

Chelsea thought about describing some of the haunting images that rose unbidden from nowhere and clung to her consciousness like burrs: bloody worms with toothy mouths that burst from her stomach, razors slicing her eyes, flames engulfing her body and burning her skin black and red, the poison that would make her swell up and die, or the tractor trailer that would crush her chest as she biked home from work or school.

But she wanted to keep her job, so she said, "You ever afraid there's a monster under the bed, ready to grab you?"

The girl's eyes narrowed. "Maybe. Sometimes. Yeah."

"My OCD tells me that unless I do certain things, like count, the monster will get me."

"But that's stupid. Monsters aren't real."

"Yeah," Chelsea admitted. "It's very stupid." Dr. Gambinetti said it was good to be aware of how irrational the OCD's demands were.

"Is it like a voice in your head?"

"More like a strong feeling. It's a part of the brain that doesn't think so well. It just thinks about survival. It's like a reptile brain. . . ."

The girl's eyes brightened. "A reptile brain?"

"In a way . . ." Chelsea began, but before she could explain, the girl was hurling herself down the aisle, hitting chew toys and dangling leashes with her shoulders as she ran and sang, "Mommy! Mommy! That girl has a reptile brain!"

It was 4:30. School was out but it wasn't dinnertime yet, so Rhett's Pets was at its busiest and at its busiest, it was packed. So of course everyone turned to stare. First at the shouting girl, then at horrified Chelsea, who wished she had told the little brat about the eye-slicing thing. Now wanting to die, she looked down, scooped more pellets into her hand and hoped the world would just go away.

197, 198, 199, 200. Finished.

She put the bowl into the aquarium tank. The warm scent of mammal and wood shavings hit her face as she lay the meal down inside. Rather than eat at once, the rabbits continued to stare at her as she slapped the pellet dust from her hands and stood up.

Even the fluffy think I'm insane.

Doing her best to pretend nothing had happened, Chelsea approached the girl and her mother. The woman's ring-covered fingers gestured from the hoop of a shopping bag toward one of six rolling pups. "The golden lab, please?"

Zach. One of the favorites, always chasing his tail, or rolling on his back. Chelsea named him after a hyper kid she used to know from group with ADD. How long ago? She was sixteen now, and she had known Zach in sixth grade, so, five years?

There she was, counting again.

The OCD had been bad since last night, ever since her boyfriend, Derek, asked her if she wanted to go to Hobson Night, the town-wide college party. Part of her wanted to go, but old lizard-brain insisted it would mean rape and death, not necessarily in that order.

A wire mesh covered the top of the puppy box. If she didn't count all the squares in the wire, all the puppies would stop breathing.

No. No, I won't do it. I won't count anymore.

She lifted the puppy into her arms, trying hard not to look at the rows of wire squares. "Hey, fellah! How you doing? How's my Zach?"

"Zach's a stupid name. I'm going to call him Zilbowser," the girl said.

The wire formed a grid. If she counted just one row up and down, she could multiply to get the total. Maybe that would be good enough.

8, 9, 10, 11 . . .

No!

She turned her back to the squares. Sweat broke out on her forehead as she carried Zach to one of the little rooms where the girl and her mother could sit and play with him. As she walked, the feeling rose.

You're killing that puppy! You're killing it!

An image flashed in her head—her throttling the puppy, grabbing it by its feet and smashing the little girl in the face with it.

Shut up!

Chelsea wiped her forehead, put the puppy down with the women, and went back and counted the wire squares.

Eight by sixteen is one hundred and twenty-eight.

Another failure to report to Dr. Gambinetti. Maybe it was because it was midterm week. Maybe because it was winter and the days were getting so short. Low serotonin levels supposedly influenced the disease. Maybe it was just Hobson Night. That always got to her too.

Thankfully, Pete emerged from the storeroom with a sheepish grin on his pimply face, ready to take over for her. Now all she had to do was count the crickets for the reptile cages and in half an hour she'd be off for the afternoon. At least she was *supposed* to count the crickets. She could handle that. It was natural.

"Chelsea?" The familiar voice was slightly surprised. At first she didn't recognize the slight, dark-skinned woman it came from. The poised, smiling face seemed as horribly out of place in a pet store as a concert pianist at a circus. The face more rightly belonged in school, in front of a chalkboard full of tightly written biology notes.

"Ms. Mandisa," Chelsea said back. Good thing she'd caught up on all her homework during lunch that day, so she could talk cell metabolism if need be.

"I'd no idea you worked in a pet store," she said. "How exciting." Her large brown doe-like eyes sparkled. With her confidence, the slight accent Chelsea could never place and her worldly air, Ms. Mandisa, as far as Chelsea knew, was the opposite of OCD.

"Yeah," Chelsea said. "I like animals."

Geez, I sound like I'm three years old. Maybe I should make some animal sounds for her too. I like the cow. It goes moo.

"I know. I'm an animal lover myself," the teacher said. "It's what you want to study in college, yes?"

Chelsea nodded. "I want to major in animal behavior at the University. I . . . I'm sorry about that first test."

She'd erased the first paragraph a thousand times,

22

until the rough paper was as thin as onion skin.

Ms. Mandisa shook her head. "Don't be silly. Your essay was the best in the class. You just should have told me about your condition sooner. That which does not kill us makes us stronger, no?"

Unless it maims you.

"In fact . . ." The slight woman scanned Chelsea's face. Chelsea felt an awkward urge to count the long seconds they stood there, but before she began, her teacher completed the thought.

"I'll be leaving early for winter break, heading home before it gets too cold. Never did get used to the snow."

Chelsea was disappointed. Not only was Mandisa her favorite, this meant a sub would be there for the midterm, someone new she'd have to explain her "condition" to, in case she needed extra time to finish the exam.

"Point being, I'll need a pet sitter while I'm gone. Someone interested in animals."

Chelsea brightened immediately. "A dog? A cat?"

Mandisa's eyes twinkled mischievously. Her lips tightened into something between a grin and a frown. "A little more involved. It's a bit of a challenge. I'll need someone I can trust to do everything just right."

That was Chelsea. The OCD made sure of that. "Okay, so what is it?"

Mandisa's eyes flared. "Something wonderful, really. Amazing. It's a . . . good-sized monitor lizard. Koko. That's his name. You see, before I came to Bilsford to teach, I was a herpetologist in Egypt, in a small research facility in a city called Kom Obo. Mostly we studied crocodiles, but I specialized in monitors. I had seven in my lab. They're the most sophisticated lizards in the world. Smart as dogs, really. Probably smarter. There was this one who stood out as really different, really wonderful. I just couldn't give him up no matter how hard I tried."

Chelsea fought an urge to count the fluorescent lightbulbs. "Didn't some guy get eaten by his pet monitor?"

Mandisa's sparkly laugh at once made Chelsea feel foolish and at ease. "That was four years ago in Oregon. He had six full-sized water monitors, let them wander around his apartment freely and hadn't fed them in over a month. When he died of a heart attack, they just did what came natural. And that's probably the only story you'll find about a monitor attacking its owner. Ten or fifteen people a year are killed by dogs. Even more by domestic horses. Koko is well fed, gentle, and in a very, very secure cage. I wouldn't even expect you to take him out. You'd just have to feed him and make sure his temperature's regulated. I'd pay you three hundred dollars for the two weeks, and if you want, you could write a little paper on him for extra credit in class. Just the kind of thing that would look good on a college application."

"Umm . . . thank you. Thank you so much. I'd have to talk to my parents."

"Of course. Have them call." She scribbled a number on a piece of paper, handed it to Chelsea, smiled again, and turned to leave.

Chelsea stared at the number. She counted the little blue lines, counted the pen strokes that made up the numbers. She'd lied. She didn't have to ask her parents. They'd be thrilled at her doing something even a little risky. Her father, Ben, would anyway, and he'd talk her mother into it.

And she was sure Ms. Mandisa would make them think it was safe.

And of course it was.

But still, she counted Ms. Mandisa's elegant steps as she exited the pet store, afraid that if she didn't, her teacher might lose both her legs.

Derek chomped on a cheese fry, its thick end dark with barbecue sauce. Though sixteen, same as Chelsea, he still hadn't quite gotten the hang of closing his mouth when he chewed. Strands of what looked like bleeding potato were visible between his teeth. It made Chelsea think about what she might look like in the mouth of a lizard.

As he ate, he talked. "What do you think Restrooms will say?"

"Restrooms" was Derek's clever nickname for her shrink. Three years of Italian class, starting in middle school, had left Derek with one word, *gabinetto*, which meant "washroom" or "bathroom." Derek found toilet humor hysterical. For a while, poor Dr.

Gambinetti was "Restrooms" Gambinetti, Mafia hit man. Time and boredom (Derek and Chelsea had been seeing each other six months) shortened it to "Restrooms."

"Dr. *Gambinetti* will say it's a great opportunity," she said listlessly. "A perfect chance for me to challenge myself."

It was after her shift at Rhett's, before her weekly therapy appointment. The two of them sat in a coffee shop, surrounded by Bilsford University students with their heads buried in laptops or books.

Derek nodded vigorously, remembering to be supportive. "It is! Definitely. It's like kismet. I don't understand why you'd even think of saying no."

"Hello?" Chelsea waved her hand in front of his face. "Big, old house. Big, old lizard? Can it get creepier?"

"Sure," he said, munching more fries. "It could be two lizards."

Chelsea closed her eyes. Of the 30,368 residents of Bilsford, 19,878 were students enrolled in the University. That left 10,490.

Derek read her face. "Are you doing it right now? Counting?"

"No," she lied, but she couldn't look at him. She

poked her Caesar salad and fought an urge to count the croutons. "I just don't want to be there alone with something that might eat me."

Derek brightened and managed to look cute, despite the dollop of sauce on his lip. "That's the beauty part, L. C. Big, old, *empty* house. Who says you'd have to be alone? You could be with me!" He took a quick slurp of his soda. "It'd be like having our own place for two weeks!"

She raised an eyebrow at her boyfriend. Derek was sloppy but sweet, and into digital photography. He was cute and very understanding about the OCD, but he could also, on occasion, like many boys, approach her with all the subtlety of a mastiff in heat.

He leaned forward across his orange plastic tray. "You'd be crazy to pass that up."

"First of all, I *am* crazy. Second of all, we wouldn't be alone. There'd be Koko. A monitor lizard. Same family as Komodo dragons. Ever hear of them? They can grow more than ten feet long and attack and eat *horses*."

"Come on, L. C. Restrooms says you have to fight harder!"

"I *am* fighting!" she said, eyes flaring.

"Oh yeah? How many fries have I eaten?"

"With or without the barbecue sauce?"

"I *always* use sauce."

She shook her head. "You scarfed three down before you could peel the lid off the packet. Since then it's been thirty-two. I can't . . . I can't help it."

His tone softened. "I know, I know. Fine. Forget about Hobson Night. Forget I ever asked to come over. Forget about us. This is important for you. It's what you want to do, right? You love animals. And a monitor lizard? What could be cooler, L. C.? This lizard, it's part of the cycle of life."

He called her L. C. for short. It had something to do with El Cid, a hero of some sort. Ages ago, when he first came up with the nickname, it'd seemed adorable, like Restrooms Gambinetti. "It's like me eating the fries that fall back from the rest of the herd." He scooped up a handful. "I do not eat out of anger or malice, but only because I must feed."

He stuffed them all in his mouth at once. Little bubbles of white burst from the golden brown. She couldn't help but laugh.

He swallowed, then tried to look serious. "You can't let the OCD stop you from realizing your dream, can you?"

Chelsea sighed.

"What's wrong?"

"That's exactly what Dr. Gambinetti is going to say."

"Score one for Restrooms," Derek said, popping his fifty-sixth fry into his mouth. "You can't go around the rest of your life being afraid of everything."

But Derek was wrong about that. She could, she really could.

At age eight, Chelsea washed her hands thirty times in a row then stood on her bed in stark terror, eyes wide, and refused to move for two hours, because everything, everywhere, except for the one little spot on the old green blanket where she stood, was contaminated and would kill her. A few days later, she was diagnosed with obsessive compulsive disorder.

Three months earlier, she'd visited her grandmother on her deathbed, seen her cancer-withered face, witnessed her shallow, troubled breathing. Her mother, Susan Kaüer, was convinced that this foolish decision to let Chelsea say good-bye to her nanna was what caused the disease. The visit had overwhelmed poor Chelsea, broken her.

But doctor after doctor said it could have been anything, real or imagined. Some OCD sufferers reported that their symptoms began the first time they saw the Wicked Witch of the West in *The Wizard of Oz*. It could have been a dead animal in the street, a scary face on Halloween. A nightmare. The reptile brain saw it all as real.

Her mother never believed that, just as she never believed Chelsea was one of the lucky ones. But she was. She never missed school and did well in most classes. It didn't stop her from making friends or having a part-time job. It just kept her almost constantly frightened.

Some sufferers, on the other hand, couldn't leave their homes. For others, the OCD was an early sign of Tourette's syndrome. The first time she heard that, Chelsea felt her head twisting, wanting to twitch. That was part of the OCD too. Suggestibility. It could latch onto any thought and run with it until it was something horrid. But Chelsea was never even medicated, though Dr. Gambinetti held it out as a possibility if she didn't manage to overcome the compulsions on her own.

And today she didn't seem able to overcome anything. Once she left Derek, the OCD roared for the entire bike ride to the square, old brick house in the center of town that held his office.

What if that gas pump leaked and someone tossed a cigarette down and all the cars and the people burst into flames?

She counted the parking meters in front of the building.

What if you scratch yourself on a rusty needle and get one of those infections that are resistant to antibiotics?

She counted the steps up to the white door and walked inside. The building was old, creaky, typical New England, but everything was painted white and there were lots of windows in the waiting room, so it was too bright and sunny to think of it as anything but cheerful. Though the OCD tried.

What if Dr. Gambinetti was killed by his last patient, a serial rapist who's waiting for you inside the office?

The magazines on the table. *8, 9, 10.*

Finally, Dr. G. opened the door and, barely looking at her, motioned her in. The fuzzy teddy bear of a man hummed as he swiped his rumpled tweed jacket back, adjusted his Snoopy tie and sat in his old swivel desk chair. As usual, he flipped through the massive piles of papers on his desk, humming cheerfully as he looked for her file.

As she walked in and sat on the old green couch, she realized she'd never seen him find that file. It was like a little performance for her sake, a distraction, just like the toys scattered about for his younger patients; the interesting wooden dollhouses, the muscular monster dolls. She'd been a child when she started seeing him, and back then she'd always liked his office and all the toys. The cacophony of objects, rather than being irritating, seemed to form a safe buffer against the rest of the world.

But she wasn't a child any longer. She worried for a moment she'd outgrown his ability to help her, but as he continued to hum, she noticed something new above his desk. A little strip of leather was tied to holes in either corner of a flat stone, the strip held in the wall by a red thumbtack. On the stone, he'd painted, in homey, so-so calligraphy.

WHAT MIGHT BE ALWAYS OWES
ITS DEEPEST DEBT TO WHAT IS.

"What's that supposed to mean?" she asked.

He turned from his papers then followed her eyes back to the plaque. "Oh that. That. Something I read somewhere, or maybe I made it up. What do you think it means?"

"I haven't got a clue."

"Not at all?"

"Nope."

"Okay. So. We think OCD may be physiological, based in the basil ganglia of the brain, but it's also a disease of the imagination, right? It uses your imagination to conjure horrible images and bizarre solutions. We don't want to defeat your imagination, it's a wonderful thing. But we want the OCD to let go of it. So, what's stronger than an imagined fear? Reality. So, focus on what's real, not what you feel might be real. Reality would exist without our imagination, but imagination would not exist without reality. So . . . get it?"

He pointed at the stone and then turned back to her, apparently giving up on pretending to find his notes.

"Sort of."

"Well, maybe it's not a very good quote. But how was the week? Where's the OCD at, right now, on a scale of one to ten?" His chair squeaked under his weight as he leaned forward in it.

"Twelve."

His eyes widened. "Really? That's high. What's going on?"

She shrugged. "Midterm week is coming up and I'm doing a double shift at the store. Derek asked me to go to Hobson Night."

He nodded. "Of course, of course. Pressure gives the OCD an in, but remember it can't do anything except scare you. What was that project we had from last week? A book you started but couldn't finish, because if you did you'd die from some infection?"

The Missing, by Sarah Langan. She was sorry she'd ever heard of the damn thing. "I finished it. I couldn't put it down. It's about a virus."

"And?"

"I couldn't sleep for two days."

"But what happened? Did some virus come out of the book and infect you?"

She shook her head. "No. It was fiction."

"So who's in charge, Chelsea? You or the OCD?"

She shrugged. "Me?"

"You don't sound sure."

"Me."

"So. Thoughts can't hurt you and you're in charge. Now, I can't advise you to go to Hobson Night. But if I could advise you to go . . ."

"I know. I just . . . I just don't want to."

He made a face as if he didn't believe her and then looked at her, a little puzzled.

"So, what are you not telling me?"

It was a common-enough question, but this time it happened to hit the nail on the head. In a few short, clipped sentences, she repeated the offer from Ms. Mandisa. As she spoke, his smile spread into a grin. "Wonderful. But you're afraid of the lizard?"

When he said the word, she thought she felt something twitch in her skull, like a flashing tail. Reptile brain. Lizard in my brain. Chelsea nodded.

"I can understand that. They can bite. They can scratch."

"It's more than that. Monitors can get really big. And they're aggressive."

"Is this a big lizard?"

She furrowed her brow. "I don't know."

"Okay. Is it in a cage or is it wandering around the house?"

"A cage. Ms. Mandisa said it was totally safe. She used to study them. She was a herpetologist."

"And we trust Ms. Mandisa?"

"Pretty much."

"So there's a good opportunity here for you, but you're worried there'd still might be some danger. What's the OCD telling you to do?"

"Don't do it. No matter what. Don't do it."

"And what should you do?"

"Go and see if it really is dangerous before I decide."

The doctor nodded. "Yes. Exactly."

He pointed at the little quote above his desk, and for a second, Chelsea felt as though she understood it.

On the outside, at least, the home of Ms. Mandisa was disappointingly unremarkable. It was a typical white cape, sort of stately if you accepted a loose definition, dormers extending the second floor headroom. Maybe it had been painted once in the last ten years, but the lawn was overgrown and the rust on the chain-link fence was worse than Pete's acne. A blue Volvo was planted in the yard, the fraying Bilsford High School parking sticker looking like its newest part.

Not that it was unusual. Most academics weren't big earners, and—head in the clouds anyway—some just let their places go to seed. What bothered Chelsea more was how far she was from home. The bike ride that she'd told her mother would take fifteen minutes was closer to forty. Thirty-seven minutes, eighteen seconds. And she was cold despite her warm jacket.

Chelsea pedaled onto the gravel driveway. She hopped off, laid her bike against a thick pine and noticed that all the first-floor windows were barred. This was also not unusual. The university town suffered from many a petty robbery. Usually no one was hurt, but there was always some down-and-out student willing to test your doors or windows. The newer colonial Chelsea shared with her parents had a full-blown alarm system, but her parents had only installed that so she could sleep at night.

She looked up and thought the bars on the second-floor windows were pushing it. Bilsford thieves didn't bother to climb. Too much effort. She made a quick circuit around the house, counting. Twenty-one windows, all barred.

Back out front, a cheerful yipping made her turn to see a creature from a fantasy story galloping straight toward her. She gasped at the little brown body and white mane. Except for the floppy ears, it looked like a tiny horse. She thought she was hallucinating until she recognized the dog's breed: Chinese crested. They'd had one just like it at Rhett's when she started there. Pete nicknamed it "Ming the Merciless" because of the way it shredded chew toys. This little fellow had the same coloring.

Wait a minute. Could it be?

"Ming?"

The dog yipped again and lolled its tongue. It was Ming! Chelsea bent and patted the tiny horsey head, noticing the dragging leash. "You're a surprise! Yes you are! A nice surprise! Where's your owner, baby, huh? You got a tag?"

She felt around the neck and pulled a pink collar with silver studs into sight. Could it get more tacky? Well, what other sort of person would want a dog that looked like a little horse, anyway?

"Aristotle!" a sandpaper voice cried out. Chelsea remembered the tall, elegant woman who'd bought the dog two months ago as she strode up on her long legs. At five foot ten, she was a sight to behold. Straight, bleached-blonde hair dipped below her shoulders. Straight bangs hung over plucked eyebrows and eyes so blue, they had to be contacts. The light colors she wore, faded jeans and white turtleneck, coupled with her pale skin made her seem fragile, like porcelain.

"Bad, Aristotle!" the woman said. To Chelsea: "I'm

so sorry. He's so frisky. Just a puppy!"

"It's okay. I know him. I work at Rhett's."

The woman's mouth rounded with recognition. "Yes. I remember. You kept counting the change, like it was going to be different each time." She scooped the little dog into her arms and nodded at the house. "You live there?"

"No, my teacher does. Ms. Mandisa."

"Hope she's hiring you to mow her lawn."

"Sorry. Just pet sitting."

"She has a dog?" the woman said, surprised.

"Uh . . . lizard."

"Ew," she said reflexively. "Well, if you need anything, or if Aristotle gets loose again, I'm Tess Sullivan. I live right across the street." The woman spun and walked toward her box-like home, the long leash dragging behind them.

Turning back, Chelsea crept up the leaf-laden path to the door of the cape and tried to avoid counting her steps. There were only four stairs leading up to the porch, though, so she took them in at a glance before she could stop herself.

It wasn't really an OCD thing. More an observation. Perfectly normal, right?

Before she could press the paint-covered buzzer, the

door opened, revealing Ms. Mandisa. She wore a brown housecoat with orange accents that matched some of the dead leaves, and a wide grin that was singularly hers.

"I was afraid you'd decided not to come, and then I saw you with my neighbor. Quite a character, isn't she? Come in, come in."

As Chelsea entered, Ms. Mandisa lingered at the door, fidgeting with a big lock that seemed, strangely, to have a key on the inside. "The door's a little complicated," she said. "I'll explain all that later, so you don't lock yourself in."

The door had opened to a staircase heading up. To the right was a small hall leading deeper into the house, a single doorway on the side. Further right was the living room proper, open to the hall and stairway. Outside the afternoon sun was shining, but the living room was dark enough for a small lamp to be turned on. Thick green drapes smothered the windows. The flower-patterned couch looked expensive and foreboding. Chelsea, afraid she'd have to sit on it, scanned for things to count.

But Ms. Mandisa kept walking, down the hall and into a wide, sunny kitchen with a back door. Chelsea followed her hostess, sliding her windbreaker off as she went. She was sweating already, and the house felt very warm, steamy even. Old radiators pinged and hissed.

"Juice? Coffee?"

"OJ with water would be great, Ms. Mandisa."

"Call me Eve. Just not in the classroom, all right?" she said pleasantly.

Chelsea nodded and sat, not at all sure she wanted to call her teacher Eve. She liked the way *Ms. Mandisa* felt when she said it, but now, of course, the woman might be hurt if she didn't use her less-lyrical first name. The table she sat at was a massive thing that looked like it could stop a tank, but at least it was clean. Though there wasn't a spot of rust or decay, the design was very retro; silver edges, thin silver legs and a white Formica top. In the pattern lay scores of swirling dots, like instant coffee grains melting in hot water. The urge to count them was strong, but she resisted.

"Mostly I live in the kitchen. The living room is so depressing. I only go in there at night to read," Eve Mandisa said as she retrieved the juice from the refrigerator.

"Why not take off the drapes?" Chelsea asked, quickly adding, "Eve."

Eve made a face that revealed her skin was not as

smooth as Chelsea thought. Tiny crow's-feet stalked her beautiful eyes and mouth. "The bars are more depressing than the dark. Mrs. Tenselbaum, the last owner, was a shut-in. Spent the last decades of her life without ever stepping outside. Sad, isn't it?"

Chelsea assumed Eve was fishing for her to say something about her own condition, but it was a bad tack on a few counts. Shut-ins generally had agoraphobia. OCD could strike anytime, anywhere. It didn't matter where she was. Still, there were days when she felt like locking herself in her room.

"Emily Dickinson was sort of a shut-in," she answered defensively.

She heard the juice pour from behind the open refrigerator door. "Would you really want to be Emily Dickinson if it meant never going outside?"

Chelsea shrugged. "Well, yeah."

Eve raised her head above the fridge door, smiled and shook it. "I guess you like her poetry more than I do. Mrs. Tenselbaum didn't write anything except checks. All the window bars and locks she put in would be ridiculously expensive to replace."

She put the juice in front of Chelsea. Throat dry from the cold outdoor air, Chelsea drank greedily.

"Upstairs is my bedroom and a lot of junk. I'd

rather you didn't go up there. Not that you would. Everything you need is down here anyway. You can put your coat in the hall closet if you like."

Stay downstairs. Check. But then, where was the big, bad lizard? She twisted her head back toward the hallway, scanning, wondering if she'd missed a cage or a terrarium in the shadows of the living room.

"So where's Koko's cage?"

Eve's face broke into a grin. She raised her hand to her mouth in a gesture that looked like she was catching a laugh before it escaped. "Sorry, I should have explained. It's not a cage, exactly. Koko's habitat takes up most of the basement. The only part of the house that has my special touch. Had to have the whole thing redone, special heating, infrared lights and such. That's really why I couldn't afford to remove the bars from the windows."

Chelsea reared, noticing the remaining door in the kitchen that must lead to the basement. "Whatever he's in, he can't get out, right?"

Eve laughed and this time didn't bother to stifle it. "Of course. Koko's smart, but there's no way he's getting out, unless he charms you with his cute eyes and pouty expressions. Ready to see him?"

Chelsea nodded, even though she wasn't. Eve rose.

45

"First the gross part. Get through this and I promise the rest is a snap. Koko only eats every other day, and I leave tomorrow." She stepped toward a second, larger refrigerator Chelsea hadn't noticed before.

Her eyes shot to the tabletop. How many dots were there? *6, 8, 10, 12 . . .*

Eve bent over and took something out of the fridge. Not wanting to seem like a complete idiot, Chelsea forced her head up. Eve held a large plastic bag in her hands. There was something in it heavy enough to make the bag sag, wet enough to cause a reddish liquid to pool in the bottom seam. Interior moisture blurred the surface, but white and brown fur was visible.

"Rats," Eve said. "I buy them prepackaged. It's amazing what they do these days."

Wanting to look at anything except the horrid bag, Chelsea's eyes scanned the kitchen, but there was no comfort to be found. The two refrigerators were crammed on either side of a large gas-burning stove. She'd hated gas stoves ever since that propane truck exploded on the interstate. The article said the whole back of the truck flew across the earth like a missile, crashing through three houses, setting them ablaze before coming to rest and starting a forest fire.

Immediately, the OCD assured her that the same fate was in store for her.

Nerves increasing, Chelsea turned back to Eve Mandisa and, try as she might to stay riveted on the woman's pleasant face, could not help but take in the bag again. This time she made out their little noses, whiskers and long hairy tails, curled like wet string. There were three in the bag, eyes closed. One had its head shoved into a corner, reminding her of a sleeping rabbit.

Seeing her reaction, Eve lowered the bag, making it easier to ignore. "You don't need a psychological condition to be disturbed by this part. It is gross. But if you're serious about pursuing animal studies, it may be something you want to try getting used to. It is the hardest part, I promise."

Eve took her hand and pulled her to standing. "Come along and let's see Koko. He's really quite fascinating."

Counting quickly as she could, Chelsea stared down at the table top (12, 14, 16, 18) as her teacher pulled her gently along, deftly hiding the bag at her side. "It's okay."

They stepped toward that door in the far kitchen wall. Eve opened it and a blast of hot, moist air hit

Chelsea in the face. She stared down and saw gray-painted wooden stairs curving left. A yellow light from below traced a semicircle on a dark wood-paneled wall. Eve started down, and then looked back at Chelsea.

"Are you good?"

Chelsea nodded. She had to do this. Had to, if she didn't want to be stuck the rest of her life, afraid of the echoes in her own brain. So she followed Eve down, counting the steps, trying to guess their height in inches and the depth of the basement in feet. She had trouble with inches, but over the years she'd developed an unerring eye for exactly how long a foot was. Each step was less than a foot tall, maybe eight inches. And by the time they reached the last one, she knew there were twelve.

Twelve steps in all.

All painted.

All gray.

She was about to count the height of the ceiling in feet, when a surprise, a pleasant one for a change, took her aback. The moist heat had intensified, but at the base of the stairs, rather than harsh concrete or the fiery pits of hell, there was a nice, clean sand-colored carpet.

She looked up and felt as if she were standing in a zoo.

No windows, yes, but light and heat were every-where. Occupying most of the basement was the cage, or the habitat, as Ms. Mandisa had called it. Three quarters of the space was sealed off with thick Plexiglas walls five feet tall. Some kind of chicken wire led up from the top of the Plexiglas to the remaining three feet of ceiling. There was a Plexiglas door in the middle of the biggest wall with strong bolts holding it shut, and near that, a small round window that looked like it opened. Chelsea assumed it was for putting in the food.

On the far side of the clear plastic was a whole other world. There were thick vines, a tree trunk, patches of grass and other plants, as well as a small pool of gurgling water. A hissing made Chelsea think she'd spotted the lizard, but the sound was coming from some sort of humidifier that sprayed mist. Three powerful lights hung in the ceiling above the enclosure, shining on the water like small suns. The back walls, beyond more wire and Plexiglas, had been painted to look like the sky.

Intrigued now, Chelsea scanned the little jungle for signs of animal life. In a corner not far from the circu-lar window was a huge, thick pile of leaves, twigs, and what looked like straw. Poking out from the pile, quiet as you please, was Koko. His head, anyway. The rest of his body was hidden in the pile.

He—it—looked . . . cute. His flat, broad head was huge, tapered to a snout. His lips were curved where they met in a way that made him look like he was smiling. Black, as if all pupil, his eyes were small and set beneath a ridge in his clay-gray skull. They looked intelligent somehow. Maybe it was the smile.

He rested his lower jaw on the back of one five-fingered claw. The way he just lay there, lazy, smiling, with that human-looking hand of his, he looked sort of like Kermit the Frog. Or perhaps a distant cousin.

Eve and Chelsea stood in the smaller section of the basement reserved for humans. There, recessed fluorescents glowed in a hung ceiling and light oak paneling covered the walls. It, unlike the rest of the house, was tasteful.

"See, he's not so bad, is he?"

Chelsea shook her head. It was like looking at one of her nature books, only close up. The OCD warnings had faded and she found herself pleased to be seeing this amazing thing.

"How big is he?" she asked, stepping closer to the Plexiglas.

"Five or six feet, last I measured. But that's mostly tail." Eve rapped on the Plexiglas with a knuckle of her right hand. "This was the most expensive part. Three inches thick, but he could have dug through drywall or even wood with those claws of his, and I'd have spent my entire life replacing walls."

Chelsea looked again at the thick "hand" Koko rested his head on, this time noticing the sharp, thick claws. "He tries to get out?"

Eve shook her head. "Not really. He's pretty happy, but any intelligent creature gets a little antsy now and then. I couldn't risk him wandering off in the winter. He'd die in a few hours in the cold. And they're not stupid. Monitors are the most advanced lizards on earth. They can recognize individual faces. Koko even knows the sound of my voice, don't you Koko?"

As if in response, the big head flicked out a forked tongue. Chelsea was startled by the sudden movement. It proved Koko was really alive.

"Ready for the big event?" Eve asked. Not waiting for a response, she walked over to the circular opening and grabbed something long and metal leaning against the wall. Then she set the plastic bag on the floor and withdrew one of the rats. Shed of the wetness inside the bag, it looked less gross, as if it really were just sleeping. "I'll do the first, you do the next two, okay?"

Again, Chelsea wasn't given time to respond. The metal thing Eve had grabbed, about six feet long, she noticed, had some kind of mechanical claw. The bio teacher grabbed the dead rat with its business end, lifted it, slid the little window open, and pushed the long arm, rat dangling, toward the darling giant Kermit head.

SNAP!

Chelsea barely saw Koko move. One minute the rat was dangling in front of him, the next, it was gone, Koko was chewing on something, and Eve was withdrawing an empty metal claw. When Koko swallowed, apparently not bothering to chew much, a rat-sized lump appeared in his throat and shortly disappeared.

Chelsea was repulsed, terrified, and fascinated.

"Your turn."

Chelsea turned to her teacher, not bothering to wonder exactly what sort of shock was on her face. *What are you, out of your freaking mind?* she wanted to say, but she didn't. Instead she made a little squeaky sound in the back of her throat.

Gently but quickly, like an impatient mother, Eve reached out and pulled her closer. "Come on, come on. Please. I couldn't find anyone else. Chelsea, if you can't do this, I'll have to cancel my whole vacation, and I've never been picked up by a limo before. Please. It's not so bad. I swear. Just try."

Chelsea let the woman guide her a few steps closer, let her put the metal thing in her hands. It was heavy. Heavier than a baseball bat or a rake. She noticed scratches at the end and a few dents. Teeth marks?

Eve held up the open bag. "You don't even have to touch them with your fingers. Just use the claw to pull one out."

Trying not to shake, Chelsea maneuvered the claw end into the bag. It worked pretty easily. In seconds, she snagged one of the two remaining rats and hefted it. It dripped a little as it came free of the bag.

Chelsea thought she would puke, but Eve was thrilled. "That's it. That's great. Just put it into the window and reach it toward him. Koko will do the rest."

Eve slid the window open and even pulled the claw closer to the hole, as if she were guiding the efforts of a child. The woman was so calm, so certain, Chelsea felt a little stupid as she stuck the claw deep in the habitat toward the big head.

"Talk to him. That way he'll recognize you when you come again."

She cast her teacher another glance, then said, weakly, "Hey, K-Koko. Here you go, fella. Nice . . ."

THUNK!

The bite was so powerful it nearly knocked the metal pole out of her hands. It didn't feel like a living thing at all had touched the pole—more like it had been hit by a truck. Chelsea opened her eyes wide and, eager to get it over with, as if the claw were her arm, started quickly pulling it out as Koko chewed and swallowed.

Eve slowed her. "Not so fast. Don't want to drop it. If you do, there's a spare here, but sometimes I use it to clear out the crap if I don't want to go in. If you have to, you can use it to get the first pole back, but clean it with bleach before you feed him again. And don't lose both of them. I don't have a third. Come on now, one more and we're done."

Chelsea made that involuntary whining noise again, but managed to fish out the last rat and stick the claw back in.

THUNK!

She was done. With a sense of accomplishment she carefully withdrew the claw again and laid it against the wall. Eve was beaming. "Great! Just great! You did it!"

Chelsea was feeling pretty good about things, but then Eve stepped closer to the clear wall. She laid her forehead against it, watched Koko chew and said,

"You know, if you think about it, it's not a bad way to go."

Chelsea's face scrunched. OCD or not, that was a creepy thing to say. "What do you mean?"

"You're young, maybe you've never seen anyone die slowly from cancer," Eve said. "I guess I think it would be like giving yourself over to a greater intelligence rather than something that just doesn't care."

"My grandmother died from cancer."

"Oh . . . I'm sorry."

"It took three weeks, but I don't think we ever considered feeding her to a monitor lizard," Chelsea said. Then she stepped away. She wasn't so much offended as freaked, but she used her indignation to mask that, a trick she'd done many times before. Only her parents and Dr. Gambinetti knew her well enough to call her on it.

Eve sounded abashed. "I am so sorry. I only meant that it was quick and seemed merciful."

The explanation didn't help. Chelsea started backing toward the steps, but Eve stopped her.

"Just a few more things," Eve said, sounding like a teacher again. "Then you can go." She indicated a set of thermostats and dials on the wall. Next to them a printed sheet with instructions and phone numbers had been posted. "The entire system is automated, so there shouldn't be any problems, but when you feed him, just check to make sure that the temperature and the humidity are at the right levels. He also needs all three lights on during the days in order to digest, and the UV light so he can produce vitamin D3. Maybe you can do a paper on that for your bio project! If anything goes wrong—anything—there are phone numbers here for you to call."

She turned to Chelsea. "Okay?"

"Got it," she answered, but she was already at the base of the stairs. As she started climbing, she could swear Koko lifted his head slightly to follow her movements, and flicked his long forked tongue.

Chelsea counted the twelve steps going up, grabbed her jacket from the kitchen table and headed for the front door. The rush of victory had faded, replaced with the image of her grandmother being eaten by Koko. The OCD was screaming:

It'll get you. It'll tear the flesh out of your legs. It'll rip open your chest.

None of which seemed terribly unreasonable. To keep it from happening, she looked at the staircase heading up from the front hallway and furiously counted the steps to the second floor. She stopped at eight, turned to the door, twisted the handle and pulled. It was locked. The key was missing from the lock. She felt her heart begin to pound.

Eve came up behind her, a chain of keys dangling from her hand. "Another gift from the shut-in. All the doors work like that. I think she was terrified she might wander outside while sleepwalking or something, so she locked herself in every night. Here."

Chelsea took the keys in her hand. They looked worn. The labels on them were old and difficult to read.

"This will be your set while I'm gone. I was going to have new ones made, but this is the set the former owner gave me. They work. Just don't force the wrong key into the lock, it might snap when you try to get it out."

Chelsea nodded, and in an extreme act of self-control, slowly found the right key, inserted it in the lock and pulled open the door before ever so gently pulling the key back out. The cold air, so much colder than the basement or even the living room, sobered her, but not much.

"Sorry if I got a little nervous, there . . . Eve," she said as she stepped onto the porch. "I'm working on it."

Eve lingered at the door, leaning her head against its edge, regarding her carefully. "I know. I could see how difficult this was for you and I'm sorry if I said anything stupid, but it is terribly important that you come back every other day for the next two weeks. You will do that, won't you? Bring a friend with you if need be. And if for some reason you absolutely can't, call me. I'll have to fly back. It's my first vacation in ten years, but if that's the way it is, that's the way it is. Okay?"

Chelsea caught her breath, feeling terrible. "I'll do it," she said. "I promise. Really. It wasn't so bad. And he looks kind of like Kermit."

Eve smiled, but her eyes still scrutinized Chelsea. "He does, doesn't he? Good, then. I believe you. I'll see you in two weeks."

She shut the door, but as Chelsea walked down the four steps and mounted her bicycle, she felt eyes on her. Eve's from the window? Or Koko's?

It'll rip you apart.

Just a lizard in a cage. Just a lizard in a cage. She repeated it over and over, then counted the number of times she said it. Her throat was so dry. She stopped at the end of the block and entered a small convenience store. There she stood counting the bottles of

Coke in the refrigerator until finally she started to feel a little better.

"Yeah?" a gruff voice said. She turned to see a fat fifty-something man behind the counter. He had hair stubs everywhere, not just on his face, but even on his neck. There was so much fat around his face, his eyes were like slits. Normally he would have set off her OCD, but it was already roaring, and he did at least look better than a lizard that could swallow a rat in one gulp. A little better anyway.

"Dasani, please," Chelsea said.

"A dollar twenty-nine," he said back. He had a watery voice that almost sounded like a gurgle. She pulled a crumpled five from her pocket and handed it over. He gave her the bottle, but before she could open it, he handed her the change, almost all of it in quarters.

"I'm out of singles."

She stared at the coins. *11, 12, 13, 14* quarters. 1, 2 dimes. 1 penny.

The owner watched as she counted them again, and then again.

"What's the matter?" he said. "Don't you trust me?"

That was the problem. She didn't. She didn't trust

the man whose eyes vanished into the folds of his head skin. She didn't trust the change. She didn't trust the water. She didn't even trust the world not to open up and swallow her whole, like a giant, merciful lizard.

Heavy and sticky, the fear lingered like a wet, suffocating blanket, through the day, into the night. Scant moments of sleep were filled with dreams of feeding crickets with human heads to the Rhett's Pets chameleon, and pinky mice that looked like human babies to the milk snake.

Chelsea even woke up afraid.

Over the years, she'd been taught tricks to free herself of the more lasting terrors, to breathe slowly, to try to think of something else long enough for the bad image to "get bored" and go away, anything to lower the continual stream of adrenaline coursing through her body.

It was evidence of the existence of free will, of mind

over matter, that she could, if she tried, make it work. She'd done it before, the first time when she was twelve. After passing a cemetery, she'd been frightened for hours that she'd become like a ghost, invisible forever, unable to touch or be touched unless she counted each and every telephone pole in the city. The dread rose like an ocean tide inside her, drowning her, but finally she was so heartsick of being afraid that she managed not to count at all. The feeling passed in about fifteen minutes, the average time it takes a human body to shed its rush of adrenaline.

But invisible ghosts—that was a girlish fantasy. She'd gotten pretty good with the really silly things. The damp, dead rats in a bag, bred to be food, were real. The feel of the mighty jaws snapping against the metal claw as if it was her arm, was real. And monitor lizards, sometimes, really did eat people, like that guy Eve told her about, who died and his monitors fed on the corpse. She Googled the details and learned that even the victim's father wasn't surprised by the fate of his son. He really hadn't been at all careful with his pets.

That should have been comforting, but it wasn't.

Dogs and cats had been known to do the same, but they didn't scare her the same way. Why? A big barking dog could make Chelsea jump, but it never set off her OCD. It was their eyes, she decided. They were different. Their faces shone with emotion. They were mammals, after all. They had limbic systems, feelings. Koko, as much as he looked like a Muppet, was more a machine, eyes dead, no matter what Eve Mandisa said about his sophistication.

He had crocodile eyes that shed crocodile tears.

Chelsea spent the day at school trying to think of anything but her new babysitting job. She had two midterms, Spanish and math, and her traumatic encounter with Koko had the unexpected side benefit of making the tests seem easy in comparison. She had something called a 504 in place in case she needed extra time to finish a test, but this time, she didn't have to use it. Mr. Abbaté grinned and patted her on the shoulder when she handed in the trig test with ten minutes to spare.

After that, she pretended to be tired, giving her an excuse to avoid Derek and her friends. She really just didn't want to tell them about Koko, so she wouldn't have to conjure the images she worked so hard to bury. She even took the afternoon off from the pet store, a little mental-health afternoon that she deserved anyway, so she could wander through the center of town, look in the bookstore windows, and try to shed the last of her fright.

It wasn't a great December day for a walk. It was colder than yesterday and a strong wind yanked the few clinging leaves from the bone-fingered trees. The grass on the commons, stiff but not quite frozen, crunched beneath her feet. The only thing that looked warm were the billowing clouds in the big, blue sky, and they were too far away to afford any comfort. But she walked anyway and, after a while, felt normal—comfortable in her skin. The world felt normal. Winter was coming, yes—but that was normal.

She also finally realized that while Koko was real, her fear of him eating her was just as much a fantasy as becoming invisible. The imagination could do many wonderful things, but it could not ever predict the future.

By the time she returned home she felt stupid and embarrassed. Not because of the OCD—there was nothing she could do about that—but for not talking to her friends. If not Derek, who might make fun of her in his efforts to help, at least she could have spilled her reptilian guts to Lori and Delina.

In a massive effort to exorcise her demons, she typed out the whole story, full of all the details she could remember and posted it on her MySpace blog.

It was difficult, conjuring the giant face of Koko and the sight of him chewing, but in the end she succeeded. With a strong feeling of self-satisfaction, she posted the entry.

It was with even more pleasure that within twenty minutes, she watched the messages of support come rolling in, some from friends at school, some from her therapy group, others from people she knew only as silent voices online.

> You go, girrl!—Numnuts90
> That is *so* brave! :-) Jason340
> The only lizard you really have to worry about is your reptile brain! Beat it back to the prehistoric age where it belongs! I luv you!—Lori
> Now that u conquered mount monitor, wanna go 2 Hobson Night?—Derek

And so on. She leaned back in her chair and looked at the laptop screen, terribly pleased with herself. She felt like she'd survived some horrendous catastrophe, like Hurricane Katrina, instead of just making it through a training session for a part-time job. It was something she learned in therapy, small steps, small triumphs. She was feeling calm, not even thinking about the day after tomorrow, when she'd have to go back there again.

So what was the antidote to fear? Knowledge. Since the computer was booted up and some more messages might come in, she decided to open another window in her browser and Google some more about the devils themselves, monitor lizards. She was surprised at the wealth of information and the huge number of lizard fanciers.

There were many species, from the dreaded Indonesian Komodo dragon, the ten-footers that ate everything from water buffalo to each other and were known to dig up fresh human graves for a snack, to the *Varanus brevicauda*, which only grew to about the size of a human finger, tail included. In between, there was the nile monitor, the crocodile monitor, the desert monitor, and the Australian lace monitor, which could grow as long as the Komodo, but wasn't as heavy.

But which was Koko?

Their heads tended to look the same, and now Chelsea was sorry she hadn't plied Eve Mandisa for more information. Monitor owners (who sometimes called them "companion animals" rather than pets, which Chelsea found a little creepy) all talked about their habitats, but none seemed quite as nice or as big as Koko's. They mentioned the right temps, the dead rats for the larger lizards.

The most common "pet" monitors were the Savannah monitor and the Nile monitor, both of which could grow to be more than six feet. Maybe Koko was one of those, but his skin didn't quite match the olive brown of the Savannah or have the distinct yellow bands of the Nile. There was a larger water monitor that could grow to nine (!) feet and a rare Australian Papuan, the longest lizard in the world, rumored to be able to attain lengths of up to fifteen feet.

She felt a little tickle, asking her to count. *6, 9, 15.* She looked at her room and measured the distance. Six feet was as long as her bed. The image of a lizard in there, waiting for her, flashed in her head, but she beat it back. Nine feet was nearly the width of her ten-by-twelve room. But fifteen feet—something that long couldn't even fit in here. Unless it curled up and waited for her. The Komodos, she read, would hide in the brush, take a bite out of their prey—a big bite—and then wait for it to either bleed to death or succumb to the venom in its saliva before feeding. Scientists used to think Komodos had filthy mouths full of bacteria that would infect their prey. It was only recently discovered that they actually did produce venom.

Chelsea looked at her leg and pictured a chunk of it missing down to the bone. Pictured it starting to rot while the lizard in her bed just waited, biding its time.

She snapped her head back to the screen.

The other thing a lot of the sites mentioned was how safe the monitors really were, how intelligent and interactive. The big water monitor was so popular because it was so docile. Koko could be a water monitor—a nice, docile water monitor. One of the sites echoed what Eve Mandisa said about dogs killing ten to fifteen people a year. Dogs: 15. Monitors: 1.

15, 1.

What was wrong with that picture? Something didn't square with Chelsea's mathematically diseased mind. Wouldn't the real danger depend on how many dogs or monitor lizards are around? A quick Google told her there were more than sixty million pet dogs in the United States. Her OCD seized on it and pushed it to an illogical extreme.

If there are sixty million dogs and only fifteen kill someone, the kill rate is 0.00000025 percent. But if only one person owns a monitor lizard and it kills him, that makes the kill rate 100 percent!

Chelsea felt her heart rate rising. When her mother's voice at the door startled her, she felt like she would explode.

"It's amazing how far you've come." Mom beamed. She stood smiling in the doorway and didn't even yell at her about all the dirty clothes scattered around the room. She just came in and starting picking them up herself. "I don't think I could feed anything dead rats."

The word *rats* careened through the air, stuck to Chelsea's skin, and started gnawing. She had to look at her arms and legs to prove there was nothing there. She started counting the hairs on her arm, the goose bumps on her skin. This was bad. Words hadn't bothered her for about two years. She felt like she was slipping back to childhood. Slipping, hell—she was falling.

Why had her mother done that? The woman was forever finding just the wrong thing to say.

"Please!" Chelsea howled.

No. I am not going to let this beat me.

Her mother stood up straight, shocked, helpless with worry.

"It's just words. It's just feelings. The feelings will

pass," her mother said, but she sounded more like she was trying to convince herself.

Summoning her will, Chelsea swallowed and calmed herself. "Yes, I know. You're right. Say it, if you want to."

"If you can't do this, you don't have to go back there. It's *okay* if you're not ready."

"No," Chelsea said, sitting at her computer, typing away. "It's not okay. Ms. Mandisa would have to come home from her trip. And I want to be able to work with animals."

Her mother walked up and kissed her on the forehead. "You can't do everything in a day, my darling."

Chelsea was about to close her eyes when she thought she saw the blanket on her bed tremble. She wondered if the lizard in it had turned, but then she buried herself in her mother's arms. In about fifteen minutes, as her mother held her, the feelings finally passed. A few hours after that, her emotionally exhausted brain finally crashed, and Chelsea fell into a deep and dreamless sleep.

With no immediate midterms to occupy her, Chelsea got through breakfast and lunch by pretending it wasn't her first day of lizard-sitting. When the sun hung heavy in the sky and further delay would mean visiting Koko at night, she thought of asking her parents to go with her or asking Dr. Gambinetti to give her a shot of something to get her through. But ultimately, she decided, no, she'd somehow have to handle it. She would power her way through, just do it. Don't think about it at all, just go.

What might be always owes its deepest debt to what is.

She repeated it like a mantra, enjoying it more each time. Even the few OCD images that dogged her, bloody and dangerous, flitted by almost in the back of her mind. She was rested now and feeling better.

Resolute, she pulled her bicycle out and faced the wide streets. The cool air was bracing, demanding her attention, as was the bike and the road ahead. Block after block, she passed children playing in their yards. Then, entering the university proper, she swerved over and over to avoid the students that whizzed past her, driving their secondhand cars well above the speed limit.

On the other side of Bilsford University, many of the older houses, rented out to five or six students, looked like pig sties, with beer bottles lying on the porch, windows broken and signs for Hobson Night adorning the trees out front. It wasn't until the sounds of the campus traffic faded in her ears that the houses were more well kept. Still, the good feeling lasted until she saw the small corner market, with its wrinkle-faced owner, that meant she'd reached the street where Eve Mandisa lived.

As Chelsea rode up, Tess Sullivan was on her porch, wearing an impossibly bright yellow jacket, cupping her hands to her mouth and calling, "Aristotle! Aristotle!"

Chelsea didn't blame the little horse-dog for wanting to flee from that fashion nightmare. It was probably roaming a golf course somewhere, looking for a small cowboy to ride it.

As the woman continued yelling, Chelsea kept her eyes dead ahead and full of purpose. The Volvo was still in the driveway, but Eve had mentioned she was being driven to the airport by a limo service.

She climbed the steps and fished the keys from the pocket of her jeans. Finding the right one on the second try, she pushed the door in. It was again warm in the living room, but not quite as warm as she'd remembered. Eve had probably lowered the heat to save money.

Chelsea stripped off her thick coat and, not bothering to hang it in the hall closet, laid it across the couch. Then she did something she'd wanted to do the first time she was there. She pulled back the dark drapes and let bright sunlight exorcise the room. The darkness disappeared like a ghost. Even the huge couch and the elephantine lounge chair with its back to the hallway seemed cheerful. Chelsea actually smiled.

Now came the hard part. The kitchen. The refrigerator. She hesitated in the hallway, wavering, and again let herself count the steps up to the second floor. *10, 11, 12, 13.* That seemed unlucky. She strained forward and felt satisfied to see the fourteenth step. Maybe she should walk up, count again and make sure?

No, not this time. Besides, Eve said she should just stay on the first floor. She was going into that damn kitchen.

You can't! This lizard will . . .

Gritting her teeth, Chelsea stormed into the kitchen, threw open Koko's refrigerator and pulled out one of the many plastic bags inside. Her nose wrinkled and she turned her head, but she managed to shut the fridge and carry it toward the basement door. As she did, the phone rang.

She froze. Should she get it? No, she had momentum

now, the bag was in her hand, she was halfway done. If someone wanted to reach her, she had her cell. It was obviously for Eve. She did wait, though, at the head of the stairs, counting the rings until the answering machine picked up. Four. It was set to pick up on four rings.

As she heard Eve Mandisa's pleasant, perfect voice recite her phone number, Chelsea opened the basement door. The welcoming light was still on downstairs. By the time she reached the sixth step down, the machine beeped and someone was saying, "Eve, where are you?"

Probably some friend she'd forgotten to tell about the vacation. Maybe Chelsea should pick it up and tell her. No. Lizard first. Time to power through.

She walked downstairs and entered the pleasant room with its toy jungle. The moist heat again took her a little aback, but this time she was ready for it. She figured half her problem last time was probably all the temperature changes.

Still not looking at the bag in her hand, she scanned the temperature and humidity gauges. According to the printed sheet, they were all dead center in the right range. The humidifier thingy was hissing along too. Everything seemed perfectly in order.

She noticed this time that the far side of the Plexiglas enclosure fell shy of the basement wall, probably so someone could get in there for cleaning and maintenance. But how wide was the gap between habitat and cinderblock? One foot? Two?

Now, now, now . . . the lizard and the food.

Koko was still sitting on that comfortable nest of dead vegetation, mostly buried by it. She thought she saw a tip of his tail or something sticking out from one end of the pile. Most lizards, she recalled reading, are nearly all tail.

This time, though, Koko's big head was sitting lazily on two claws, making it look even more human, more intelligent than it had last time.

"Hi, Koko!" Chelsea said. "It's me. Your sitter."

Koko raised his head slightly, turned his black eyes toward her and flicked his tongue just once. Could he recognize her already? Maybe he wasn't so cold. Maybe she was just being prejudiced toward mammals.

She took another few seconds to take a good, long look at him, to try to memorize his dark clay color and the broad-snouted shape of the head so she might better compare him to the pictures she'd found online. Right now she was guessing water monitor. Big but docile. Maybe next time she should bring her digital camera, take a photo. But maybe the flash would bug him?

And how many photos could her camera hold? *32, 33, 34.*

No, no, no. Now or never.

Keeping her eyes on Koko, she lowered the bag to the floor and opened it. The edges made a sloshing sound as they came undone. Still not looking down, she picked up the metal claw.

She had to look as she lowered the claw into it, but it really wasn't so bad, just little lumps of fur in a dark pool. She snatched one with the claw, and once satisfied it was attached, again looked away.

Quickly, very quickly, she lifted claw and rat and slid them through the opening, pushing the arm out farther and farther, closer and closer to Koko, until . . .

SNAP!

She did it. A little smile came to her lips, not unlike the one Koko always seemed to have.

Thrilled at her victory, she quickly loaded the second rat and repeated the process.

THUNK!

The powerful snapping of the jaws was still startling, but she was getting used to it. She chose not to watch the chewing or the swallowing part.

Wow. One dead rat to go.

This time, she didn't bother to look away, and even used the claw to shake the rat over the bag, removing a bit of the wetness. Koko raised his head in anticipation as it came. Maybe next time she could coax him out of that nest thing and take a really good look at him.

THUNK!

Something was wrong. He'd clamped down on the metal arm. Thinking quickly, she turned it sideways and he let go at once. It'd probably just gotten stuck on his jaw.

Terribly relieved and downright thrilled, she withdrew the claw, put it back on its hook and dumped the wet plastic bag in the trash. It didn't look like Koko had messed his cage yet, so she didn't even have to use the second claw to clear it.

She was done. Totally done. Her body shook a little, but in a good way. Maybe her parents and the doctor were right. Maybe the OCD could just become a helpless little squeaky voice that she would always be free to ignore.

Before she left, she took one last look at Koko. His head had shifted from the brief tussle with the claw, revealing a bit more of his nest. Among the bit of green leaf and brown twig, there was something else, something under his chin that didn't look like it belonged. Thin and long, shredded at one end, it practically glowed against the clay gray of his skin. Curious, she stepped closer to the Plexiglas for a look.

In a second, her mind pieced together what it was and seized on the sight with its own reptile jaws.

Under Koko's chin were what looked just like the remains of a pink and silver dog collar.

Shivering, Chelsea stumbled backward, nearly knocking over a garbage pail full of plastic bags soaked in rats' blood. She raced up the stairs, grabbed her jacket and fumbled with the keys, nearly breaking the one that finally set her free.

She heard the door click behind her, vaguely remembering she hadn't bothered to draw back the drapes. But by then she'd tossed her coat over her handle bars, hopped on her bike and started pedaling, as fast as she could, past the yellow-coated woman still shouting "Aristotle! Aristotle!" past the corner shop, and past all the houses, where she counted every window, every door, in the mistaken belief it would make what she'd seen just go away.

She couldn't have really seen it. She couldn't have. Could she?

Yes. It ate the dog.

Though freezing by the time she got home, she didn't even wait for the water to heat up. She leaped into the shower and ran the bar of soap up and down her body in staccato pulses to wash off all the invisible rat and dog blood.

By the time she emerged, an hour later, Chelsea was together enough to lie to her parents about how things went. But they knew. She heard the heated whispers of their exchange. Mother wanted to pry, but Dad insisted they hew to their agreement to let their daughter sort it out herself, with the understanding she would ask for their help when she needed it.

The next day, Chelsea's parents were gone until evening, so they never found out that after they'd said good-bye in the morning, Chelsea didn't come out of her room until dinner.

5

"What do you mean you can't do your bio midterm right now?"

Eve Mandisa's substitute, a retired elementary schoolteacher named Kreeger, looked up from her *New York Times* crossword puzzle and glared at Chelsea. It was not possible for a human face to look more irritated.

She didn't say it softly. Everyone in the classroom looked up from their work. Those who knew Chelsea shuddered for her. Chelsea, meanwhile, tried to explain. She spoke quietly, to maintain some semblance of dignity, but that only seemed to irritate Mrs. Kreeger all the more.

"OCP? You have OCP? What's that supposed to

be? Some club? These are the midterms, dear. Don't take the test, you fail the class."

Chelsea made her voice louder, still hoping to keep it low enough so that at least the back rows didn't hear. "Obsessive compulsive disorder. It's in my file. I'm allowed to delay or reschedule the test if I have to. And I have to."

The older woman strained to make sense of her words. "Allowed? I don't know where your file is. Just sit down, please, until the time is up."

"Ms. Mandisa keeps our files in the upper right drawer."

Mrs. Kreeger looked around as if she might actually open the drawer, but apparently decided it was too much trouble to push her chair away from the desk and bend. "Maybe you should just get yourself some water and try again. Everyone gets nervous now and then."

Chelsea wavered, but held her ground. "This is different."

As if affronted, Kreeger tossed the *Times* crossword puzzle down on the desk and turned her wide, frumpy body toward Chelsea. "You're not a child anymore. What are you going to do when you have some real pressure in a job?"

Chelsea stared at her. "Get fired, I suppose."

She didn't say it meanly. Didn't even mean to be rude. Thankfully, something in Kreeger recognized that. She grunted, opened the drawer and asked Chelsea her last name. Chelsea spelled it as she pointed to her file. A summary of the 504 was taped to the front, the important details highlighted in yellow. Chelsea felt a surge of profound love for her bio teacher, even if the woman did have strange tastes in pets.

And her pet had stranger tastes still.

Kreeger blasted air through her nose. "Fine. I guess it's not up to me. You're excused. But I'm not going to be the one sitting here when you retake the test whenever you please."

Thank God, Chelsea thought as she nearly ran out of the room.

Kreeger was saying something else at her back, but Chelsea didn't bother to listen, she just raced into the long, empty corridor, rubbing her temples and trying to stop her heart from hammering. When running felt silly, she put her head against the cool tile wall, trapping bits of blonde bangs between it and her skin.

Then she practiced her deep yoga breathing.

She hadn't told a soul about her last visit with Koko, but the image of the pink dog collar sitting under those big, hand-like claws burned inside her, so hot, it felt like it would sear through her forehead and come dancing out into the air in front of her.

Why had the first question on the test involved a pink line on a bar graph? It was bio, for pity's sake, not math! And why *that* shade of pink? She thought she might get away with the test, but once she saw the color, once her mind pronounced its name, it was all over. Was it the same shade as the leash or had she imagined it?

She pulled out her cell phone, flipped it open, ignored the message alerts, and considered, for the twentieth time, dialing the local police. She'd looked the number up so many times, she put it on her speed dial. It wasn't a 911 call, after all. It wasn't like they could pull Aristotle back out.

And what would happen if she did call? What would happen if she told some world-weary desk clerk that the monitor lizard she was taking care of had eaten a dog? Could she sound sincere or sane enough to get them to pay attention? And if someone met her at the house and she brought them down to that basement room, and it was all true, what would happen to Ms. Mandisa? Was it legal to keep a six-foot, dog-eating lizard?

Beyond that, what if it wasn't true? What if the lizard hadn't really eaten the dog? It didn't make sense, after all, and the lack of sense was a major warning sign that the OCD was in charge, yanking her crank. That she really was crazy.

With all the windows barred, Aristotle couldn't have gotten into the house, let alone the cage, and with all that thick Plexiglas, Koko couldn't have gotten out. So was it really a leash she saw? It was entirely possible, calm and happy as she'd been at that moment, that she'd imagined it, that the light from the heating bulbs caught a stick or leaf in just such a way that her mind contrived the rest.

That had to be it. Aristotle was probably safe at home right now this very minute in the arms of his fashion-challenged owner. Had to be.

Sigh. It was the same damn conversation she'd been having with herself since yesterday, the same talking points, over and over, only instead of counting the books on her shelves, or the Cheerios floating in her milk, now she was counting the tiles on the Bilsford High School walls.

The reason she kept going around with it wasn't her condition. It was the conclusion. It was always the same, and it was the one thing she longed to avoid most of all. If she couldn't be certain of what she'd seen, she had to go back and figure out whether it had really happened or not. She had to take another look, and maybe even use the claw to pull out the thing that looked like a leash, to make sure it wasn't.

An image flashed, pieces of Ming—of Aristotle— still attached to the collar, coming out from under Koko as she pulled. Koko grabbing the metal arm and pulling Chelsea through the small hole, so that he, with his lazy Kermit grin, could more easily feed on her.

124, 125, 126 tiles.

She wasn't stupid. She wasn't going back by herself. She had to bring someone with her, just in case it was true. Someone who didn't think she was crazy. Someone who would just help.

Someone who wouldn't tell anyone else if I asked.

Derek.

He was at school this morning, but Chelsea didn't know which test he was taking. She did know, like she knew the length of the back of her hand, that inevitably he'd head to the cafeteria for a snack. There were no classes. The school was only open for the midterms, so she was free to head there at will.

A powerful smell of cleaning fluid and sour milk

blasted her face as she opened the double doors to the huge cafeteria. That and the fact that the huge room took up most of the basement reminded her of Koko's habitat. Keeping herself under control, she scanned the sparsely populated tables and didn't spot him anywhere.

It could be hours before he showed, but was she in a hurry? Should she be in a hurry? If Chelsea was wrong, it didn't matter at all. And even if she was right, did it matter *when* Tess Sullivan found out her pet was dead?

Two of her closer friends, Tony and Darlene, a couple for six months, sat at a corner table, so Chelsea walked up to join them. Unfortunately, they were sitting with Penny Denning, a junior who made no secret of the fact that she wanted Derek. Penny's gray sweater picked up the girl's black hair and smoky blue eyes. She looked positively predatory, even had a half grin on her face.

The three were chatting excitedly until Chelsea walked up. Then, all of a sudden, on seeing her, they clammed up.

She rolled her eyes. "You heard I had to leave the bio test, huh?"

They all looked puzzled.

"No," Tony said.

"You had to leave the bio test? Are you okay?" Darlene said. Darlene had become horribly sympathetic to the pain of others now that she had her own boyfriend. When she was single, if she was on her cell phone, she'd walk right past you if you were bleeding to death.

"Eep," Chelsea said as she sat down. "Guess I didn't have to mention *that* then, huh?"

"Guess not," Penny said.

"But are you okay?" Darlene repeated.

One of the ways OCD kept victims in its grip was by getting them to keep secrets, to lie and say they were fine when they weren't. Her parents and Dr. Gambinetti had worked with her for ages, getting her to talk about it as much as she could, keep it all out in the open. Still, Chelsea didn't feel like announcing her insanity to any group bigger than one, and certainly not to Penny.

"I'm fine. Just having a bad day. Bad weekend. I'll take the test Thursday. The sub was a royal bitch," Chelsea said. She twisted her head sideways. "So what *were* you guys talking about when I walked over?"

"Nothing," Tony said. He was a crappy liar, too.

But Penny spoke up immediately. "We're all going

to Hobson Night at nine. Some of the college kids have made a sluice out of carved ice and they pour vodka down from the top. You sit on a chair at the bottom and drink as it comes down."

"Penny!" Darlene protested.

Penny shrugged. "She asked. She's a big girl. Am I supposed to lie?"

Darlene rolled her eyes and offered Chelsea a soupy grin. "We didn't want you to feel bad, because, you know . . ."

"Because my OCD won't let me go, right? It's okay, Darlene. I'm fine. Who else is going?"

Darlene fumbled, but Penny picked up the ball. "Everyone. It's like a celebration for finishing midterms."

"Not Derek, though," Tony said.

"Right, not Derek. I tried to talk him into going," Penny said.

I'll bet you did.

She looked at Chelsea. "But he wouldn't. Not without you."

Chelsea couldn't help but smile a little.

"You think that's cool, don't you? You shouldn't be so selfish. Just because you can't bring yourself to go because you're too afraid of being raped and mutilated doesn't mean you should hold him back. Is that fair?" Penny said.

"Penny!" Darlene said again.

Chelsea winced, not just because the words brought the image to mind, but also because Penny was right. Derek was dying to go, but he wouldn't go without her.

Just as Chelsea was achieving a whole new level of feeling bad, Derek walked up. "L. C.!" he said. "I've been emailing, IM'ing, text messaging, and calling your cell. I was thinking of actually writing you a letter. Why've you been blowing me off? You leaving me for the lizard?"

She walked up to him, wrapped her arms around his neck, and gave him a big kiss. From somewhere behind her, she could hear Penny huff in disapproval.

Derek smiled. His eyes actually wobbled a bit from pleasure. "Okay, I forgive you." But as he focused on her face, he knitted his brow. "You okay?"

"Can I talk to you in private?" Chelsea whispered.

He nodded, so she led him off to a quiet corner of the cafeteria.

At first she spoke in halting tones, but then, as she told him everything she'd been through, she spoke faster and faster, until finally she was making one very long sentence connected occasionally by the word *and*.

When she got to what he considered the most interesting part, he couldn't keep from bursting into a grin.

"So you think it actually ate a dog? Wicked!"

"Shh!" she said. "This is *so* serious! How can you laugh? It's horrible!"

But the fact was, she wished she could laugh too. Then she might be able to do something about it herself. Maybe that was why she stayed with Derek. So many things that seemed awful to her struck him as laughable. It was a strength.

"Come on, L. C., it *is* funny! It's probably just a twig or something, like you said."

She sighed. "I have to go back to see, to make sure. Come with?"

He didn't hesitate. "You bet! I'm done with my tests and my car is outside. We can go right now."

At first she thought he was just being an amazing boyfriend, but then she realized he was really excited about seeing the cool lizard that ate the dog.

As Derek pulled up, Chelsea noticed that the trees lining the street all had posters on them. She knew what they were for before she even got out of the car to look, but she felt compelled to see for herself. In big black letters, above a color photo of a Chinese crested, it said: HAVE YOU SEEN MY DOG?

Not a good sign. Aristotle wasn't safe at home as she'd hoped.

The temperature had dipped yet again and the cold made her cheeks ache as she stared at the picture of the little dog. She glanced at Tess Sullivan's house, saw her at the window looking out, but didn't dare turn to face her. Instead she tried counting the branches on the tree.

"It's groomed to make it look like a little horse," Derek said coming up behind her. "Freaky." He was munching on some chips from the open bag he'd found in the backseat of his car. She heard them crunch between his teeth as she turned again to the picture of the dog. *Crunch. Crunch.*

Like Koko's jaws, moving.

It was true. It had to be. She felt as if she was going to tumble into an abyss inside her own mind, fall forever. But when she shivered, Derek put his hand on her shoulder and brought her back to the world.

"Come on," he said, clacking his tongue against the inside of his mouth. "Let's check out Koko."

On the porch she fumbled with the ancient keys. Derek stood there in his thin jacket, slapping his hands against his legs. He was trying not to hurry her, but he was clearly freezing. She stopped for a second and turned to him, "I'm sorry about Hobson Night. Maybe you should go without me. I know Penny wants you to."

He looked up at the gray sky. "Penny? Nah. They say it's going to snow tonight anyway. Maybe you can come over to the house and we can watch a DVD or something."

She smiled a little, knowing what "something" translated to in his hard-wired male brain. Finally, she managed to push the right key into the lock. They stepped in, Derek strutting ahead as if he owned the place. The first thing she noticed was that with the drapes open, it was lighter but drafty.

"So where's the reptile house?"

Chelsea tugged half-heartedly at a thick drape. Maybe she could leave them open until Ms. Mandisa came back.

"Downstairs," she said weakly. "The basement door is in the kitchen."

As they walked down the hall she could see it was open, like she left it, the yellow glow visible against the bottom half of the door. The last thing in the world she wanted to do was the only thing she had to do: head back down there. Maybe she could send Derek alone. No, that would be stupid. Selfish, just like Penny thought. Besides, then she'd just worry that Koko would get him.

She neared the door and stopped short. "Wait."

"What?" Derek said. He knew her well enough to add, "Come on, let's just get it over with."

Feeling like a child trying to avoid an injection at the doctor's office, begging for just a few more seconds, she switched tacks. "I'm supposed to feed him today. We have to feed him."

It was a good idea, anyway. If they were going to poke around his nest with a mechanical arm, better Koko should have his tummy full.

"Great! So are the rats next to the brewskis?" Derek said. She'd told him the story, so he walked right over to the fridge, popped it open, and started ferreting around in it.

He emerged a few seconds later, a look of boyish delight plastered on his face. "Whoa!" he said, dangling one of the plastic bags in front of him. "Check it!" He shook the bag so the rats sloshed in their juices.

Chelsea turned away, feeling like she was going to

throw up. Gritting her teeth, she led him down the steps, counting the slats in the paneling. As they entered, she realized that, though the room still looked pleasant enough, since she'd thought about it so much and so often, it now held an eerie glow in her psyche, as if it were haunted.

Ignoring all the dials and instructions, Derek walked right up to the Plexiglas. "There it is, in the corner! Wow! It looks plastic," Derek said, scrunching his face. "Are you sure it's even real?"

Koko had shifted back to lying on one claw, and Chelsea was pleased to see that the collar was nowhere in sight.

"Oh, he's real, all right."

"Koko! Koko!" Derek said, rapping on the Plexiglas.

"Derek! Stop!" She pulled him back. Then a thought hit her. "So, do you want to feed him?"

Derek's face lit up, but then he looked at her suspiciously. "You want me to feed him just because you're too scared to, right?"

Chelsea nodded. "Right. Is that a problem?"

"No." Derek grinned. "Just checking."

She tried to talk him through it, but he was one step ahead of her all the way. He actually scooped the rat out with his hands and stuck it in the claw, like it was a worm on a fishing pole. She felt her lunch slosh in her stomach as he did it.

"Now I just stick it at him?"

She nodded. She was going to tell him how lucky he was that he could just do that sort of thing, but then he made a weird mechanical humming noise as he pushed the claw through the small window in the Plexiglas. *"Gshhhhhhhhhhhhhhhh!"*

THUNK!

Derek's eyes lit up. "Awesome! And you get *paid* for this?"

She took the claw from him. "You're right. I should be doing it."

"No, no! It's okay, really. I'm here. Let me. You get to do it for the next ten days!"

She, of course, feeling stupid, relented, and he repeated the process twice. Each time Koko bit, Derek's eyes lit up. The last time, he chuckled out loud. He looked at the bag again and seemed disappointed it was empty. Trying to maintain some of her dignity, Chelsea at least grabbed the wet bag and tossed it in the trash.

"So, I'm not seeing any leash," Derek said.

"I don't see it either," Chelsea said, walking up to

the Plexiglas. "But he was in a different position."

She watched Koko closely. He chewed a few times, as if savoring the last bite, then swallowed. When he was done, he leaned forward and brought his second claw back out under his chin.

And there, under his arm, she saw it again.

The angle was different, so she wasn't quite sure what it was, exactly, but the little bit of pink was obvious. Maybe it was a piece of a plant?

"There!" Chelsea said, pointing. "Right there! Under his claw."

Derek was beside her in an instant, lining his head up with her pointing finger. "That? The little pink thing? That could be anything. It might even be a piece of rat."

"Thanks for the picture, Derek. I'll keep it forever."

"Sorry."

"I saw more of it before. I just wish I could be sure. . . ."

"No problem," Derek said. He grabbed the claw again and pushed it through the window.

"Derek, don't poke him!"

"I'm not going to poke him, I'm just going to grab that little pink thing. *Gshhhhhhhh!*"

Koko raised his sleepy head as he saw the claw

coming. He eyed it warily, as if aware he'd had his three rats already and there were something unusual about this fourth intrusion into his domain. *Could lizards count?* Chelsea wondered.

Koko followed the end of the metal pole with his head all the way back to the window. Then he seemed to stare right at Derek's face.

Derek noticed. "*Gshhhh!* Easy, fellow. Nothing to see here. Move along."

For now, the lizard did nothing, only watched, seemingly bemused as the claw edged closer and closer to the little pink flap—and finally snagged it.

"Got it!" Derek said, terribly pleased with himself. "I'm a regular 'Crocodile Hunter'!"

He tugged gently, pulling it free from the straw and twigs that lay around and above it. Luckily, it wasn't actually under Koko. Luckily, the lizard seemed to find this all terribly interesting.

The pink thing swung forward, right in front of the lizard's bemused face, into the light, where it could clearly be seen. There was no question now: It was a dog collar, pink with silver studs, torn and frayed at one end, as if it had been chewed.

Chelsea screamed, long and loud, hurting her throat and filling the quiet space with a shrill, terrified sound. Koko snapped at the metal arm, yanking it from Derek's hands. It fell onto the floor of the habitat, one end near Koko's mouth, the other just below the circular window. Then Koko pulled himself completely into the shadows of the nest, disappearing, except for the tip of his tail.

"Damn!" Derek said, working his index finger in his ear as if trying to dislodge Chelsea's scream.

"He ate Aristotle! Koko ate Aristotle!" Chelsea sobbed as she sank to her knees. Her OCD, oddly enough, was completely silent, as if basking in its success. No need to say, "I told you so."

Derek tried to pull her back up to her feet. "Come on, L. C., come on. The good news, I guess, is, it's not your OCD playing tricks on you."

"What's wrong with you? How can you be so calm? This really *is* terrible!"

Derek shrugged and hugged her. "Shh. Calm down. I guess I never liked small dogs much. I mean, I'm sorry, I guess, but it happens. For that matter, how *did* it happen?"

He gently pulled away from her, helped her back down to sitting on the floor, and looked around, scanning first the floor and then the ceiling. Finally, he pointed.

"There."

Chelsea looked and wondered how she had missed it before. Wondered how it'd been missed ever. Above the Plexiglas wall, the wire mesh that ran to the ceiling straddled a basement window. It was open, not all the way, but enough. It was barred, too, like all the other windows, but the bars were far enough apart for a small, curious dog to squeeze through.

"Aristotle probably felt the warmth down here and wanted to check it out. He climbed in, fell into the habitat and . . . *thunk!*" Derek said.

"Oh God, oh God," Chelsea said. "What am I going to do?"

"For starters, call Ms. Mandisa and see what she says. I'll find something to block that window closed so we don't lose any neighborhood cats," Derek said. He had a commanding, confident tone she'd never heard from him before.

She wanted to say something nice, but instead only nodded and flipped open her phone. As she searched for Ms. Mandisa's number in her contacts list, Derek found a piece of wood just the right size and managed to wedge the window shut.

"That wire's strong." He grunted as he shoved it into place. Chelsea, meanwhile, found the number and pressed the call button. After a few moments, an answering machine picked up.

"Ms. Mandisa, it's Chelsea. Please call me right away. Something terrible has happened," she said. Then she clicked the cell phone shut.

Derek looked at her. "Way not to sound panicked," he said.

"At least she'll know to take me seriously," Chelsea answered. She managed to get to standing. In a weird, sick way, she was relieved. It was all someone else's problem now. Ms. Mandisa would probably have to fly back and deal with her unhappy neighbor and maybe the police. She wiped her eyes and felt terrible for Aristotle, but remembered what Eve Mandisa had said about it being a merciful way to go. Somehow she didn't think Aristotle's owner would be comforted by the thought.

But then she opened her eyes and noticed her boyfriend sticking his arm into the habitat, trying to retrieve the fallen claw. She wanted to scream, but the words stuck in her throat, finally coming out instead like a raspy gasp, "Derek, stop! What are you doing?"

"Relax, it'll take a second. . . ."

But before he could finish, something raced out of the nest, something very long and colored a dark clay gray. Chelsea's mind flashed back to what she'd read about the way Komodo dragons hunt, hiding beneath the brush and lashing out when prey came by. Maybe Koko hadn't been lazing under there at all. Maybe he'd been hunting.

Derek saw it coming too and pulled his arm out, falling backward in the process. It was a photo finish as the big lizard, a blur of head, body, and legs, slammed into the Plexiglas wall, shaking the whole thing, then swerved and with a flurry of shredded plants, vanished again into the back of the habitat.

Chelsea screamed again. She didn't get much of a glimpse of Koko—he was visible only for seconds, but he seemed huge, way bigger than six feet. Derek was on his knee grabbing his hand.

"Crap! Oh crap!" he said.

Had Koko bitten his finger off? His hand? What if he came back again and smashed down the whole wall?

Chelsea stumbled away and leaned against the banister, her back to the whole scene. All at once she realized that what she'd seen in her boyfriend wasn't bravado at all. It was total, complete stupidity. Her boyfriend was a jackass. A moron.

After saying, "Aggh!" and "Crap!" a few more

times, he put his arm around her and gently pulled her back to standing.

"It's okay, it's okay! I was just being stupid. I'm not gonna do that again! Boy, he's *big*, huh?"

He turned her whimpering form slowly around.

He sucked the blood off and stuck his index finger out at her. "Look! Look! It's not so bad!" Derek said. "He just nipped me."

But he was wrong again. The jagged wound was horrible. It ran half the way along the length of his finger. It looked like a little piece of the flesh had just been torn off. Derek looked at her face, then back at his finger. His brow furrowed. "Hey, you're right. That *is* pretty bad. You got a handkerchief or something?"

She shook her head. "Maybe upstairs? Can we go upstairs now?"

Derek nodded. "Yeah, I think that's a good idea."

They mounted the first of the twelve steps, but before they walked up and passed the thirty-six slats of thin paneling, Chelsea glanced back at the cage. For a few horrifying seconds, she thought Koko wasn't in the cage at all, but then she saw that familiar head, the curved nostrils, the black eyes, watching her from beneath some shrubs.

Hunting her?

Upstairs in the kitchen they found a dish cloth, which they wrapped around Derek's finger. The first time, the blood soaked through, but by the third time they rewrapped it, the bleeding had seemed to slow. Chelsea wanted to pour some iodine she'd found on it, but Derek refused.

"You kidding? That'll hurt like hell!"

"Derek, you've got to go to the hospital."

He shook his head. "I'm fine, really. Look, the bleeding's stopped. How's your OCD?" He was trying to change the subject.

"It's fine. You know how when everyone really is out to get you, it's not paranoia? Same thing here," she answered.

He nodded. "Are you counting anything?"

"There are six knobs on the gas stove. Four table-spoons and one soup spoon in the kitchen drainer . . ."

"Okay, I get the picture. But look, the dog? That happened because it wandered someplace it wasn't supposed to. My finger? That happened because I stuck it into a monitor lizard's cage. No magic, right? Counting couldn't have stopped it from happening, not counting didn't make it happen, right?"

"Right," Chelsea said, but she knew she didn't sound like she believed it.

They put on their coats, opened the door, and stepped outside, into the cold. It was later than Chelsea had realized, and darkness was falling.

Posters had been plastered on the columns that supported the roof on Tess Sullivan's front porch, across the street. More hung on her front door. Sixteen in all.

"Chelsea, you should tell her."

"I don't want to. You tell her."

He looked for a second like he just might do it, but then he shook his head.

"Okay, fine," she said. "But what if she doesn't believe me? What if she thinks I'm some stupid kid making a stupid joke?"

He looked at her face, which was white with fear. "No one would think that of you," he said.

So she nodded and stepped off the curb just in time to see the woman's car pull out and head down the street. She could have waved and stamped her feet, but she didn't, and even if she had, Tess Sullivan might not have stopped.

She looked at Derek. "You could call the number on the poster, but you can't just leave a phone message for something like this," he said.

Now he was being sensitive? Now? She nodded.

"Ms. Mandisa will probably call in a few hours and tell me what she wants to do. But if she doesn't, I'll come back and tell her. Will you come with me? Back up my story?"

He cradled his hand as he nudged her hip. "Sure. I'll pick you up after dinner."

Night clouds shrouded the Bilsford sky with a clay-gray color as dark as a lizard's skin. As it thickened into blackness, drawing even more heat away from the December air, it ultimately smothered the light from even the brightest stars. But mere dark couldn't keep the town's denizens inside, safe and warm, not on Hobson Night. As Derek and Chelsea drove through town after dinner, it seemed as if everyone under thirty was out having fun.

Everyone except them.

Groups large and small wandered the grassy commons, laughing drunkenly as they tromped the frosty grass. Banners and holiday lights hung from all the streetlamps. If you peered inside the garish fluorescent-lit windows of the supermarkets and convenience stores, you could see long lines of people with their IDs—both real and manufactured—already out as they bought cases and six-packs of beer.

Hobson Street, three blocks of ramshackle off-campus student housing that lay just a quarter mile from Eve Mandisa's, was the nexus for this dying-of-the-light debauch, but the party always spiraled out from there, sucking the whole town in. University classes had ended yesterday; the campus shutdown would occur tomorrow, but this was a night when college students rewarded themselves for work well done, or drowned their sorrows over opportunities lost. It was rumored, and likely true, that Bilsford scheduled its high-school midterms during this week specifically to keep the younger kids in the town busy and out of trouble.

Like that could ever work.

Derek slowed for a crowd in the crosswalk. Among the people, Chelsea recognized six kids from her classes, singing, "We Will Rock You."

Derek caught her longing expression as she looked out the window. "Do you want to go later?" he asked hopefully. "Just for a few minutes? Just to drive down Hobson Street and look? We can drink seltzer."

Chelsea shook her head. "Bah. Humbug. No.

Maybe. I don't know. I think I just want to go home and go to sleep after this."

"Are you sure?"

She reared. "My lizard ate a dog! I'm feeling a little drained, Derek."

"Fine. Sorry. I thought the whole idea was to distract your inner reptile."

"That's the idea, but not tonight. You should go. Really. I won't mind."

Much.

"Maybe. Maybe I should."

He sounded defiant and annoyed and she didn't blame him. Who would want to be stuck with her on Hobson Night? Last year, when she was fifteen, she'd actually finished all her tests and her friends begged and begged her to sneak out and play. Her father even made a point about how the lock on the back door was broken and, hell, anyone could sneak out and join the party for an hour or two and no one would notice. But Chelsea stayed in her room, curled up under a book lamp, startled by every crashing bottle or good-natured scream.

Tonight, though, Chelsea was on her way to tell a woman she didn't particularly like that her dog had been eaten by a lizard she was sitting.

My, how times had changed.

She told her parents everything, but they didn't seem to believe her until Derek displayed his as-yet-untreated wound. Though the bleeding had stopped completely, the width of the cut looked pink and pulpy and had acquired a strange shade of green on the edge of the frayed skin.

Her mother nearly fainted. But her father, after whistling, just said, "I stuck my hand under a running lawn mower once to grab a ring. Stupidest thing I ever did. An inch in the wrong direction and I could have lost the whole hand."

Derek nodded solemnly, but Chelsea thought she saw them swap furtive glances of "manly" approval.

Her mother instantly reached for the phone to call the police, to have the killer monster dragon arrested and/or shot, but Chelsea begged her not to, at least until Ms. Mandisa got back in touch.

"It's not Koko's fault Aristotle got inside! He was just doing what a lizard does!" Chelsea said.

Seeing her daughter defend the creature that terrified her made Chelsea's mother think twice. She put the phone down, but kept her hand on the receiver for a few long seconds, for comfort's sake, it seemed. Chelsea sometimes wondered if her mother had her own OCD, but had kept all the little fears and rituals locked away inside, all her life, telling no one.

Dr. Gambinetti said that everyone had these terrifying stray thoughts, conjured by the reptile brain, and the disease was really just a question of degree. Her father actually said he had them too, but that he ignored them. Chelsea was never sure if he really did, or if he was just saying that to make her feel better. But her mother had never owned up to anything other than a concern for Chelsea that she insisted was born only out of love.

And where was her bio teacher anyway? It'd been three hours and there was no return call from Eve Mandisa. Maybe she figured Chelsea had just freaked out over the rats, so she wasn't in any rush to hear about it. Maybe Chelsea should have been more specific. In any case, when Chelsea announced her plan to go back with Derek and tell Ms. Sullivan what had happened, her mother was further tested.

"You will not go anywhere near that house!" she screamed.

But Chelsea's father took his wife into the kitchen and the two parents treated Derek and Chelsea to a muffled but heated exchange. Words like "independence" and "best thing for her" and "she's a little bigger and smarter than a dog" danced out into the living room.

Finally, the Kaüers did what they always did when they came to loggerheads over how to handle their only daughter. They called Dr. Gambinetti at home. He, surprisingly, offered a compromise between the armed guard Helen wanted and the footloose methods Ben advocated. As it turned out, the doctor was going to be in the area and could meet Chelsea and Derek at Ms. Mandisa's himself. It would be a good place, he said, to see exactly how his patient was doing.

Chelsea figured he suggested it because it was his big opportunity to see her in the middle of a full-blown attack. Despite its sloppy appearance, the doctor's office was controlled and safe. This was real life.

The university campus was impossible to navigate because of the traffic, so they had to take the long way around. As they finally exited the center of town, with its lit buildings and equally lit denizens, into the less well lit neighborhoods, she felt her reptile brain wriggling its long, sharp tail in her head, ready to perform for her doctor.

They pulled up in front of Tess Sullivan's house,

frozen leaves crackling beneath the tires. Tess's car still wasn't in the driveway, and the house was dark, its silhouette barely visible against the trees. Ms. Sullivan obviously wasn't home. Maybe she'd given up on her beloved Aristotle and, like many of the older residents, decided to flee the neighborhood for Hobson Night.

Derek shut off the engine and looked at his watch. "We've got half an hour before Restrooms gets here. What do you want to do?"

Chelsea hadn't noticed when it began, but a light snow was falling. It was supposed to get worse— dump up to six inches—as the evening went on, but right now it was just a feathery sprinkling, floating bits of sugar against black velvet. She watched the flakes land on the windshield and melt.

"I don't know," she said. "What do you want to do?"

"Well, you know what I always like to do?"

He slid his arm around her coat.

Boys. Ready to roll at the drop of a hat. They were like—what was the word?—opportunistic feeders.

She pretended not to know what he was talking about. "No. What?"

He came forward and put his lips against hers. She did not resist, tingling with pleasure as he wriggled his arms under her coat. He took her mind off guard perfectly and she was thankful. For the first time in what seemed a million years, she actually felt herself relax. Her whole body seemed to exhale. Sure, a tightly wrapped, icy little something in the back of her mind was still beating away, but maybe if she gave in to this simple pleasure, even that could melt from the warmth.

After all, it wasn't the end of the world. Just a lizard doing what lizards do. Nature. Just like this. The circle of life.

She let him put his tongue in her mouth, prod her teeth and pull her closer. It was so quiet, except for their quickening breath, that she thought she could hear the snowflakes landing. As the car windows fogged from the heat of their bodies, she heard more than that, though. She heard tree branches crack lightly in the wind. Distant laughs. Music from a car stereo.

Then scraping.

No, scratching. Like something crawling up beside the car, something that could tear through the door and grab them.

She stayed in Derek's arms, eyes closed, knowing it was just the OCD, but she counted anyway, hoping he couldn't read her mind. She counted the flashes of darkness on the inside of her eyeballs, counted how many teeth Derek's tongue touched. Counted her breaths, counted the seconds.

Eventually, Derek noticed she wasn't moving.

He pulled away and looked at her. "Look, Chelsea, don't force yourself or anything."

"I'm not!" she protested. He just looked at her and she felt like crying. "I'm sorry. I feel so stupid. I can't even kiss you. I am so damn lame."

He pulled farther back and looked out the window. "You're not. You're not lame. It's been a big day. We'll . . . we'll try again after this is all sorted out."

She watched him, thinking how wonderful he was being. Too wonderful. In fact, he seemed way too calm about the whole thing. Didn't he want her?

"Derek, how can you just stop like that? Aren't boys supposed to get all worked up?"

"Oh, I am," he said, laughing a little. "I just . . . I just want to make sure things are right between us."

She was about to grab and kiss him again, show him just how right things were between them, when a heavy tapping came at the window that made them both jump.

The wide head and bespectacled eyes of Dr. Gambinetti hovered outside the window, surrounded by shadow and snow. He was narrowing his eyes, trying to see past the fog into the car's interior.

Derek opened the door as Chelsea buttoned her long coat.

"Very sorry to interrupt," Gambinetti said. "Are you the young man who calls me Restrooms?"

Derek blanched. "Uh . . . Chelsea . . ."

"Sorry, sorry, sorry," Chelsea said, climbing out of the car. Why had she told Gambinetti about that? She was certain she'd lost Derek to Penny now.

Gambinetti laughed. "You really should see the look on your face. It's fine, Derek. I've been called much, much worse. And I'm glad to meet you."

Chelsea could see the doctor's laugh was genuine. There was a faint smell of alcohol about him, too. Scotch? Even Dr. Gambinetti was getting in on Hobson Night.

Maybe she should?

"Chelsea," he said, widening his grin. "You don't seem all that rattled by these shocking goings-on."

"Actually," she began. Deciding she didn't want to go into the details of her aborted make-out session at all, let alone in front of Derek, she said, "Nothing."

Gambinetti nodded. "Have you spoken to the dog's owner?"

Chelsea shook her head. "No. She's not in."

"I hope you understand I'm not making light of any of this. Bad things do happen. We've talked about it. But the important thing to realize is that your imagination can't predict it. When we write, when we draw, when we"—he cast a glance at Derek—"when we play, the imagination is an amazing tool. But if it says that this telephone pole is going to fall on me if I don't recite the names of all the episodes of *Battlestar Galactica*, that's something else."

Chelsea nodded. She'd heard it all before. "But you do believe me about the dog leash?"

Gambinetti nodded. "Yes, as a matter of fact, I do. But just so I can tell your parents that I checked, why don't we go inside and have a peek?"

He turned toward Eve Mandisa's house and looked as if he was going to march right on over, but then even he hesitated.

"It's in a cage, isn't it?"

Derek and Chelsea nodded. "Yeah."

The snow fell just a little heavier as they crossed the street. Unlike Ms. Sullivan's dark house, the scant light from the open basement door reached into the living room, giving the windows where Chelsea had opened the drapes a yellow aura as if someone were watching a small yellow television somewhere inside.

As they made their way across the yard, Dr. Gambinetti, apparently a little drunk, thumped along like a big bear, barely getting out of the way of the brush and piles of leaves he encountered along the way. He kept his voice cheerful and upbeat as he talked. "Fear of reptiles runs deep. It's a natural reflex, hard-wired into our animal brains. But it can be conquered. Otherwise, how could we live in the modern world, the way it is? We don't hunt, we don't gather, and there are seldom real reasons for fight or flight, not in Bilsford, anyway. But our bodies don't know that. They just do what they're built for."

On the porch, Chelsea fished out the keys and focused on the doctor's voice. It was strange to see him, to hear him talk like this outside his office. She couldn't quite decide if it made the world seem some-how safer, or his words less useful. For now, it seemed to comfort her. Her hands weren't even shaking when she put the key in the lock. She figured Derek must be bored out of his mind, though.

"Take driving. Every time you drive your car, every time you brake, see a red light, or get stuck in traffic, adrenaline rushes into your system and your body thinks it's out on a grassy plain, fighting for its life, not sitting behind a wheel. That's why road rage is so common."

She pushed the door open and waited for the two men to walk inside first. Gambinetti hesitated again, but when Derek simply walked in, he followed, smiling at the décor in the living room. Chelsea hung back at the door and flipped a switch on the wall. As she hoped, it turned on some of the lamps in the living room. But they were low, on tabletops, and cast tall shadows around the couch and the large reclining chair with its back to the hallway.

"Koko is in the basement, yes?" Gambinetti asked. Chelsea nodded as she closed the door. "Fine. Let's talk up here a moment. I want to go through a few things. Part of everyone's brain, the reptile brain, if you will, is constantly scanning the environment for threats, for food, for mates." He eyed Derek. "Yes?"

"You bet," Derek said.

"The brain sees something, a shadow, a funny-shaped branch, that it thinks might be a threat, and it sends a 'threat alert' to the brain so the body is ready."

As he spoke, Chelsea thought that one of the shadows in the hallway had moved. But no, it was just the curved back of the reclining chair projected up on the wall by the lamp. She fought an urge to count something. Seeing where she was looking, Gambinetti unbuttoned his large leather duster and sat on the chair, revealing his jacket and Snoopy tie. It creaked loudly as his bulk pressed into it, and the shadow of the chair on the wall moved just as it was supposed to.

"The brain then takes a closer look and decides whether the threat is real or not. If not, it sends an 'all clear' signal to the body, and the body calms down. In the OCD brain, the alarm keeps coming, over and over, until the frustrated brain feels forced to imagine a way to make itself feel safe again, by washing, by counting, by checking the doors it already knows are locked. Until what, Chelsea?"

"You bring your adrenaline level down by breathing and change the focus of your mind by imagining something else," Chelsea recited. Feeling warm, she slipped off her heavy coat and laid it on the couch.

"Yes. Calm the physical body with relaxation techniques, train the mind to switch subjects. If you do that often enough, you literally build new neural pathways. It's a good reality versus a bad use of the imagination."

Chelsea exhaled. "What might be owes its deepest debt to what is."

Gambinetti smiled. "Perfect."

"But what if the threat is real?" Chelsea asked.

"Then?" He smiled. "Well, then you fight or run away."

Still smiling, Dr. Gambinetti leaned back in the squeaky lounge chair, just as two massive claws reached up from behind and clamped onto his shoulders.

He was just saying, "Huh?" when Koko's broad head appeared above his own, at first looking like a comical hat. The huge shadow that lay against the wall behind him—the one Chelsea had spied and feared all on her own, without the interference of the OCD—writhed as if stretching its muscles.

In seconds the large man and the large chair were pulled backward, tumbling over, down to the floor, where they lay beneath the mighty lizard. Gambinetti's arms flailed as Koko snapped his jaws open, downward, and attached himself to a part of the therapist's body obscured by his coat and shirt. Finding the spot, the jaws shut like a rattrap; the head twisted and pulled, yanking up some large and fleshy body part mixed with torn bits of coat.

Gambinetti never even screamed. Even now his arms and legs didn't flail so much as twitch. He was breathing, but it didn't seem right. It was too fast, too mechanical. Koko, meanwhile, most of his body still hidden in shadow, climbed up and put his great claws on Dr. Gambinetti's heaving chest.

The massive lizard raised his head toward Chelsea and Derek and opened his mouth, revealing two saw-like rows of teeth. Then Koko hissed, long and loud, as if to say, "I found my dinner. Go get your own."

Things happened quickly after that.

Heeding her doctor's final words of advice, Chelsea spun, prepared to flee. She reached the door, only dimly aware that Derek was right behind her. She yanked out the keys, but her hands were shaking terribly. Finally, with the sound of harsh breathing mixing with a terrible tearing noise at her back, she found what she thought was the right one and plunged it into the lock. It didn't slide in as easily as she remembered it doing mere moments ago, but when she pressed harder it went in.

"Chelsea, Chelsea, Chelsea!" Derek shouted at her back. "Hurry up!"

The room was filling with an even more awful

noise. It sounded like it came from Dr. Gambinetti, or at least from his throat—but it wasn't a sound you'd expect any animal or human to make. It was as though someone had connected a bellows to Dr. Gambinetti's vocal chords, then stepped on it. It sounded like a wind, like a rush of water, like an engine's roar.

Chelsea refused to turn around, but she felt Derek turn.

"Oh crap," he said into the din. But then the sound was cut off, swallowed by that terrible tearing, snapping and chewing.

No longer interested in being delicate, Chelsea twisted the key in the lock. It broke off in her hand, as if the only thing attaching it to its body had been butter.

Chelsea slammed her fists into the door, crying, "No! No! No!" The voice inside her whispered, *Told you so.*

Her slamming grew weaker, then stopped. Where was Derek? She no longer felt him behind her. She couldn't turn her head or even open her mouth to scream. She pictured Koko slithering away from poor Restrooms's body, scuttling, winding closer and closer.

Count your tears and you'll be safe, the OCD said.

But she knew, really knew, that it was lying. Nothing was going to save her now.

It wasn't until she heard another hiss and placed it, not right behind her, but much farther back in the room, that she realized the lizard was *not* right behind her. Koko was either still busy with his dinner, or he had taken Derek.

Chelsea's choice was obvious: She could either stay here, staring at the door, at the little glass window in the top and the snow that seemed to be falling harder and harder—or she could turn around and see what was really going on.

She put a bit of her cheek inside her teeth—tender and rough—and bit down hard, hard enough for it to bleed. A salty taste rushed onto her tongue. It hurt, just badly enough to jolt her nervous system out of its terror-inspired catatonia, and she turned.

In their rush for the door one of them had knocked over a lamp, so the grisly sight of Koko and Gambinetti was cloaked in blessed shadow. There was light though, down the hall and in the kitchen. Derek was standing there, waving frantically at her, mouthing, "Come on! Come on!"

Had he found a way out? The door in the kitchen was locked, too, all the windows barred. Maybe she had a key, or maybe the key she'd just broken off in the lock was the one that worked the back door.

Derek was getting frantic. She wanted to run to him—really, she did, but it meant crossing Koko's path, and *that* she could not do.

Down the hall, she saw Derek heft a heavy kitchen chair, thick with white paint, as if he were hoping to beat the giant lizard to death with it. Realizing it was useless, he put it down and rifled through a kitchen drawer, pulling out one long knife after another, instantly realizing that each was hopeless for the task.

Finally, he just stood there, his hands grabbing at his hair, and could not remain silent anymore. "Chelsea! Will you run already?"

The moment he shouted, the chewing stopped. Koko's massive head reared and looked, first in the direction of Derek, just out of his sight in the kitchen doorway, then at Chelsea, perfectly visible from the living room. It looked like the lizard was deciding what direction to head in. So Chelsea ran, not toward Derek, but up the stairs to the second floor, all fourteen of them. She took them two, three at a time. There was a door near the top of the stairs, but instead of trying to open it, she whirled onto the landing and squatted behind the banister that ran along the second-floor hall, the whole of the stairs and just a bit of the landing below visible.

She felt briefly free, like an astronaut traveling between earth and the moon experiencing a few true moments of zero gravity, like maybe she had left all the horror down there, behind her, like maybe it was all a dream and she was just a little girl, fleeing her mother or father in a wonderful game of hide-and-seek.

It didn't last. She pressed her head against the wooden support posts holding up the railing and panted, marveling at how she had no control over her fast breathing. She looked down. The wobbling light from the fallen living room lamp spilled through the posts, making long, black bars of shadow against the staircase wall.

Being ever so gentle with herself, she twisted and tried to peer over the banister, straight down the stairs. She could see the frayed welcome mat and even a small bit of the living-room floor. Koko was nowhere in sight. She didn't hear any struggling, so she assumed Derek was safe.

He'll die if you don't count the posts.

She started counting. *6, 8, 12, 14.* But stopped herself when she heard a rustling sound below. A big shadow shifted in the living room. As she stared from

126

behind the railing, Koko's head appeared at the base of the steps. She could see his thick, forked tongue swiping out at the air, trying to taste the scent of fear.

She heard Derek's voice, muffled by distance as he shouted, "Hey! Get away from there!" But Koko's head kept on coming, up the steps, pulling his shoulders and his thick body behind it.

The lizard was climbing. Of course it could climb. How else could it get out of the basement? How *did* it get out of the basement? Was it something she had done? Something she'd forgotten to do? Something she didn't count?

Oh my God!

It was a third of the way up the stairs and its body still was not completely visible. As the lizard emerged and she measured it, she knew for a fact that Eve Mandisa had either been wrong or hadn't measured her pet in many years.

It wasn't six feet.

Six feet. Seven feet. Eight feet. Nine feet. Ten. And a healthy amount of tail left over.

How? How could it be that big? The only monitor lizard in the world that size was the Komodo dragon. Ms. Mandisa couldn't have one of those for a pet.

Could she?

The skin was the right color. The head was the right shape.

Was it real, or was it the OCD?

Oh God, oh God, oh God.

"Get away!" she heard Derek scream, louder, nearer.

She heard something splinter loudly. Wood? It sounded like maybe Derek had smashed the chair against the floor, to get the lizard's attention. If so, it worked.

Koko turned his head back down, toward the hallway and the sound.

No, Derek! No! It's a frikkin' Komodo dragon! She wanted to scream, but the only thing that came out was a whimper. Images of Derek, arms flailing as Koko sat on his chest, ripping out his throat, flooded her brain.

Koko turned, maneuvering the thin space with snake-like ease, and headed back down the stairs.

Derek! No! As the lizard, and then its shadow, slunk out of view, Chelsea's throat tightened as if a tourniquet were twisting around her neck. She could feel the blood rushing out of her face, feel her heart reach a whole new level of jackhammering. Finally, just as little swirling spots filled her field of vision and she was about to pass out from anxiety, the panic yielded a rational thought:

Call 911!

Shaking more than she had when she reached for the keys, Chelsea slipped her fingers into the tight pocket of her jeans and wiggled her cell phone free. She flipped it open, comforted by the blue glow of its tiny screen, pressed the three magic numbers and hit the call button, counting the four seconds until someone answered.

"Emergency services," the voice intoned.

Inside, Chelsea was thinking, *Phew!* But outside, her body would not cooperate. The words rushed out of her head, only to be clogged in her throat. What came out wasn't even a sentence; it was more like panicked breathing.

"Ahhhhh . . . ahhhhh . . . ahhhhhh . . ."

"Hello?"

"Ahhhhh . . . ahhhhh . . . ahhhhhh . . ."

An audible *tsk* was heard, followed by a clicking. In a few seconds, a recorded voice came on the line. The voice was deep, male, and obviously reading from a prepared script.

"This is John Trent, Bilsford chief of police. Hobson Night creates a number of real emergencies as well as a massive amount of prank phone calls. If this is a real emergency, please stay on the line, and we will get to you as soon as we can. If not, please do everyone in the community a favor and hang up now."

She counted the seconds. *15, 16, 17.*

Downstairs she heard more wood splinter, then a yelp of pain and what sounded like a door slamming, followed by heavy, animal scratching.

"Derek!" she shouted. She pulled herself up to her feet and stood at the top of the stairs. "Derek!"

How many seconds had she been on hold? *32, 33, 34?*

She looked down at the phone. The line had gone dead. Maybe she had accidentally hung up. Or maybe they picked up, didn't hear her, and thought it was a prank. It didn't matter.

She hit the first number on her speed dial: home. After seven rings, nothing, which meant Dad was probably on the line with Uncle Frank and not bothering to answer call-waiting.

She hit two, her mother's cell. The phone was powered off as usual, putting her into call answering after three rings. She didn't bother leaving a message, since she'd probably be eaten by the time her mother turned on her phone again.

She hit three. The phone rang. A familiar voice answered.

"You okay, Chelsea?" Derek whispered.

She exhaled at hearing his voice. "I'm fine, fine. You? I heard . . ."

"Yeah, I kinda swatted at Koko with a kitchen chair. He didn't like that much, but it got him down off the stairs."

As he spoke, Chelsea noticed he was breathing funny, not just panting, but weakly, like he was tired. He laughed a little, but even the laugh didn't sound good. "Damn, that big son of a bitch is fast, isn't it? Got me in the hand pretty bad, but I managed to shut the kitchen door before it got in. Pushed a . . . pushed a table up against it, but it was scratching at the base of the door like it was a dog or something. It almost got through. But I'm okay now, I think. I don't think Toilets is okay, though. He didn't look too good. He looked . . . Chelsea, you stay where you are, or lock yourself in a room somewhere."

She heard some scraping on the line as he spoke, as if Derek was moving things around in the kitchen. How bad was he bitten? Komodos were venomous, she remembered reading. They'd bite their prey, and then wait for them to die. Maybe that was why Koko didn't bother tearing down the rest of the door. She pictured the lizard outside the kitchen, listening, waiting for Derek to drop.

He had to get to a hospital.

"Did you try the police?" she asked.

Another laugh. "Yeah, all I did was mention a giant lizard eating people and they put me on hold, then hung up. I think Hobson Night's got them too busy to believe something this weird. My folks are gone and my useless friends are all out partying. Don't worry, though. We'll get out of here."

"How?" she said, near tears.

He slurred his words as he spoke. "It's a freaking house, L. C. We're not in a submarine, or stuck on a plane with snakes. There's got to be a way out! Smash open a window! There can't be bars on everything!"

He was wrong. She remembered counting all the windows and the bars. She remembered being very thorough. Twenty-one windows, all barred. Even the basement window that Aristotle sneaked through.

"What if we can't, Derek?"

There was silence for a moment, then, "You know why I like you so much, L. C.?" Derek asked.

It was a silly thing to say in a terrible situation, and she couldn't help but respond.

"Why?"

"Because no matter how bad things get for you, I've never once seen you give up. You get scared because of that thing in your head, you run away, but you always come back."

It was one of the nicest things anyone had ever said to her. But of course, Derek didn't know when to let go. "If I have to be trapped in a locked house with a giant man-eating lizard, I'm just glad it's with you."

"Derek! Stop joking! This is crazy!"

"I know . . . I think I'm feeling a little woozy. . . ." She heard a strange wavering in his usually steady voice. She had to get Derek to a hospital.

It wasn't the OCD talking, but it was agreeing with everything she said.

Yes! Yes! Derek will die! Count the drawers! Count the cracks in the floor.

No. A hospital. Derek needed a hospital.

She heard him moan as he hefted something, heard glass crack but not splinter, as if his blow had been too weak even to shatter the glass.

"Hmm . . . window's pretty strong, too. Or I'm weaker than I thought. But . . . you know what?" Derek said, voice rallying behind a great boyish idea. "This is a gas stove. I can blow out the pilots, turn on the burners and when the place gets nice and full of gas, hide in the basement and toss in a match. WHOOM! That'll blow a hole in the wall!"

And Chelsea thought *she* was nuts. He couldn't possibly mean it.

"Don't Derek. Don't. That's insane. You're not thinking right."

She heard him shifting, imagined he was turning the burners on, and the oven. Imagined that even now the kitchen was filling with gas. Was it real?

"I think it'll work. There's a lighter right here. Don't move. I'll blow a hole in the wall and go get help."

"Derek! Stop! Turn the burners off! You shouldn't breathe that stuff!"

The loud scratching returned, accompanied by the sound of splintering wood, about to give. "Oh crap, he's at the door again. Gotta go, L. C. See you soon!"

He hung up.

Now she heard the scratching in reality, down below in the hallway that led to the kitchen. It was loud, insistent. She also heard Derek's voice, muffled, trying to command Koko as if he were a dog. "Get out of here! Go on! Get out!"

Dizzy with fear, she looked down the stairs. The

shadows below danced furiously in tune with the scratching. She counted how many times the big tail flashed, how many scratches, how many huge splinters she imagined the claws pulling free, how large in inches she imagined the hole must be getting.

Cold sweat poured down her forehead, like the snow she saw down below, pooling along the lower line of the front door's icy window. The storm was in full swing. Between that and Hobson Night there probably wasn't a free police officer, firefighter, or ambulance in all of Bilsford.

She looked around the second floor, down the long cluttered hall, its thin-slatted wood paneling now painted white, at the array of potted plants, at the small end table with the answering machine on it, trying to find—what? A weapon? Another phone? A score of bad monster movies flashed in her mind. Maybe she could fray a lamp cord and try to electrocute Koko. Maybe she could freeze him, get him out into the snow somehow. Maybe she could count him to death.

That idea about the freezing didn't sound so bad. Koko needed heat. In fact, maybe he wasn't even hungry anymore. Maybe he just wanted to head back down to his habitat, where his heat lamps were, but he couldn't because Derek had barred the door. That made sense. Lizards only attacked for food, then they dragged their prey off to eat and digest.

So maybe Derek should just get out of the way?

She hit his number on speed dial.

"Chelsea, if that's you, I'm kind of busy right now!" he screamed from below.

"Derek, I think Koko just wants to get back to the basement!" she called back.

"Well, too bad for him, then!" Derek shouted.

The scrambling stopped. Koko had heard her voice. Maybe even recognized it, connected her with food and the warm basement. After a few seconds, though, he started scratching again.

Her cell rang. Derek.

"Chelsea, I'm going to let him in. I'm going to let him in and blow him up!" He sounded even weaker than before. The exertion was probably making the venom move faster through his system.

"No, Derek! Don't!" she screamed, but he hung up.

At the sound of her scream, the lizard stopped again.

Chelsea froze; then an idea hit her. It could recognize faces and voices, right? What voice would be most familiar to Koko?

She turned the volume all the way up on the

answering machine and hit PLAY. Eve Mandisa's voice filled the house, announcing her name and telephone number. At the sound of his owner's voice, Koko stopped scratching completely.

Chelsea walked back to the top of the stairs, near the closest door and looked down. As messages issued from the machine, the scratching did not resume.

"Eve, where are you? Let me know!"

She saw the lizard's shadow, cast by the fallen lamp, appear again on the floor at the bottom of the steps. Koko probably figured Eve could help him get back in the basement.

"Eve, I'm at the airport and your flight arrived, but not you. Where are you?"

The shadow got bigger as Koko, somewhere in the living room now, crossed closer in front of the light. Chelsea backed up against a door. The knob turned in her hands. If Koko started climbing up, all she had to do was stay quiet, barricade herself in the room and call Derek, at least talk him into shutting off the gas.

"Eve, the airline says you never even got on the plane! I'm really worried now! Did you take care of Koko like we discussed? No matter what you think of it, it's an animal, Eve, for pity's sake! Please, please call."

137

When the tip of Koko's nose appeared at the base of the stairs, Chelsea opened the door and backed inside the room.

"Eve, I'm worried sick. No one seems to know what happened to you."

It was dark in the room, but the light from the streetlamps, reflecting off the falling snow, bathed it in a soft full-moon blue. Chelsea could make out a bed and bureau, and some suitcases piled against one wall, but nothing else.

"Eve . . ."

It wasn't until she pulled the door shut and backed deeper into the room that Chelsea nearly tripped over the half-eaten body of Eve Mandisa.

As she screamed, long and loud, Koko's feet reached the welcome mat in front of the stairs.

Already pushed to its limits, Chelsea's system over-loaded. Every neuron shot bio-electric acid along the length of her body. Her heart, sounding now like a machine gun, could not beat faster. Her adrenals wept so much of their high-octane hormone into her system, she tasted the adrenaline, warm and metallic in her mouth. Panicked energy filled so much of her body that she had nothing left with which to maneuver it into useful action. All she could do was scream and stare at the lifeless thing that once housed the heart and mind of her biology teacher.

Eve Mandisa's remains lay in the semi-darkness of the room, looking much like a cross between some latex corpse from a Halloween shop and a real-life rotting slab of meat. Sullen light from the window graced the face, which had remained untouched. Eve's mouth was closed, her eyes open. Her crow's-feet vanished in death, and she looked younger. She didn't even look shocked. Maybe a little surprised. Her lips were twisted into a kind of half smile, just like Koko's. She was either pleased at her death, or it happened so quickly the Egyptian-born woman didn't quite know what to make of it.

Merciful.

The confident voice that had spoken the word echoed in Chelsea's head.

Merciful.

Chelsea remembered how once she wanted to be more like her. She didn't want to be like her at all now.

A heavy sound from the base of the stairs snapped Chelsea's attention back to the door. The lizard, the ten-foot Komodo dragon that could take down a full-grown water buffalo, was about to come up.

And she knew exactly how many steps the huge body had to climb to reach the second floor. Fourteen. Fourteen steps. All wooden. All eight inches high.

There were more sounds from outside, very distinctive, and she imagined the image that went with them. For each step, there was a light thud—probably a front foot hitting the step—followed by a lighter scratching noise, his claws scraping the wood as he pulled his body up. Koko sounded almost like a heavy bag of clothes being dragged lazily up the steps, zippers or metal clasps scraping against the stairs as it went.

Of course, she counted the steps.

1, 2. Koko's coming soon.

The OCD begged her to count everything or else she'd burst into flame. But, for the first time, the nagging, hysterical voice could not possibly make her *more* afraid.

Chelsea made sure the door was shut tight by slamming her shoulder into it. It was nice and thick and heavy, but then she remembered that the kitchen door was heavy, too, but had nearly splintered. How long would this one hold?

3, 4. Bar the door.

What was around? She pulled her foot up, trying to get deeper into the room, but something clung to it. She prayed it was the folds of her teacher's clothing and not her ravaged body. Not looking, she yanked her foot free, whimpered, and then stepped away and looked around. What could she put against the door? There were suitcases piled on the bed. They couldn't stop an angry child, let alone a monster lizard.

5, 6. Chelsea needs a new trick.

The bureau drawers were open and empty. That didn't look right. What had been going on? Her mind flashed to the messages on the machine: *"Did you take care of Koko, like we discussed? No matter what you think, it's an animal, Eve, for pity's sake!"*

She'd assumed the caller was referring to hiring a sitter. The empty bureau made it seem more like Eve had planned on abandoning Koko. But why? Why not just take him to a zoo?

Because it's not legal to own a Komodo dragon. So what do you do with it?

So she abandoned her home and her career just to avoid a fine? It had to be more. Eve talked about Koko in such glowing terms, about how different he was, how intelligent.

"I just couldn't give him up no matter how hard I tried."

There was a bay window on one side of the room. Maybe she could pry the damn bars off and jump. She raced over and tried to open it, but the wooden frame held fast.

Nearby, she spotted what looked like some sort of sculpture. If it was heavy enough, maybe she could prop it up against the door.

7, 8. It's almost too late.

The sculpture stood five feet, almost as tall as Chelsea. Most of it was a square stone base, but on top was a huge, broad lizard, maybe a crocodile, its tapered snout sticking off the edge, its body nestled comfortably on the flat top. Why would someone have a statue of a lizard in their bedroom?

Was Eve Mandisa worshipping Koko?

"There was this one who stood out as really different, really wonderful."

She'd heard of a Christian sect that held rattle-snakes during their services, thinking it brought them closer to God. It must have, whenever the things bit. She shook her hands, rubbed them together. No snake. No snake. No snake was here, no snake was coming. Snake fake. Komodo Dragon real. Not God, just lizard.

Where was Koko? Shouldn't she have heard *nine* and *ten* by now? Had Koko's advance stopped? Maybe he was tired. Maybe being away from the warm cage was starting to get to him. She strained to listen, but heard nothing.

Maybe he was heading back down to Derek. She flipped open her cell to call him when . . .

9, 10, the sacrificial hen.

Koko was still on his way. But what had happened

with Eve? If Koko killed her, he must have gotten free before the first time Chelsea fed him. She said he was smart, sophisticated. Did Koko only pretend to be stuck in his cage? And when Eve Mandisa tried to abandon her pet, did he somehow know?

11, 12, get ready to be shelved.

Where was Derek? Why hadn't he tried to lure Koko back down? Had he gotten out? Was he getting help?

13, 14, someone call the Marines!

The floor outside the door creaked. She held her breath. He'd probably just pass by, right? But then she saw the door move in the jamb, rattle the lock. She pictured his forked tongue licking at the doorknob, tasting her fear-filled sweat.

She grabbed the statue, thinking for a moment she could shove it against the door. But she couldn't budge it.

The door rattled, at first just a bit, then more and more. She heard a sound like a thick awl digging deeply into the wood, deeper and deeper, faster, faster.

As the door began to yield, Chelsea grabbed a floor lamp, yanked the cord free from the outlet and swung the heavy base at the bay window. Apparently the adrenaline had increased her strength, because her swing sailed through the thin wood of the frame and sent glass flying. A rush of cold air filled the room, followed by bits of snow.

The door continued to shred.

It's coming to eat you, Chelsea!

"Shut up! Shut up!" she said aloud as she stuck her head out the window.

The sound of her voice excited the lizard at the door. There was already a long thin line forming, the paint cracking, showing wood.

Stupid! Stupid! Don't talk out loud to the voices in your head!

The wind was freezing. Jagged glass shards lined the hole she had made. She swung again, but her strength was fading. She stuck her head out through the hole she'd made, into the snow, into the cold. Desperate, she wedged the base of the lamp between the bars and pulled, but the lamp bent in her arms, leaving the window bars intact.

No! No! I don't want to die!

Then count or wash your hands!

There was a hole in the door. She could see the tips of the claws working, like some remorseless backhoe at a construction site.

Getting a second wind, Chelsea slammed the base of the lamp against the bars, again and again. She could see the screws that held them in place start to give at one corner, but it would take time and more strength for her efforts to make any difference.

And even if she'd had the strength, her time was up. Koko's head and front legs were wedged through the door, his claws on either side of his face as he tried to pull his body through. Long, sharp shards of wood flew or fell as the lizard made its way.

"Help!" Chelsea screamed out the window, but her voice was muffled by the snow and it didn't look like anyone was on the street. They were all at Hobson Night, drinking vodka from a giant ice sluice, where she should have been, where Derek should have been.

She thought briefly she might climb out and wedge herself between the window and the bars, but that would just leave her cornered, make her an easier morsel to chew.

Skin growing numb with cold, she pulled herself back inside.

"Derek!" she screamed.

Koko hissed at her as he pulled the rest of himself inside.

Close up now, with only the bed between them, Koko looked all muscle and sharp claw, covered by thick gray hide, too big, too hungry. It was death on four legs, more terrifying than bursting into flames or being bitten by a rattler or poisoned by touching rabbit food, or even being raped and cut up. It was more horrid than anything her OCD ever could have conjured.

And it was coming toward her.

Pulling away from the window, the lamp still in her hand, she used it as a brace and climbed atop the lizard statue. Balancing against the wall, she managed to stand on its back, her sneakers a full five feet above the ground.

Koko thudded up to the statue's base and looked up. Snow from the window flecked his clay-gray face. The little specks of crystal ice melted on his body. The black eyes stared at her, recognizing her, boring into her soul, as if they saw exactly who she was and what she was worth—just a piece of meat, just dinner.

Chelsea was hyperventilating, each breath matching her heartbeat. Maybe she was safe up here. Maybe, even though he could climb stairs, he couldn't get up this statue.

But of course he could. Koko raised his back, forked tongue flicking from his grinning lips. His front claws grabbed either side of the stone base. His long back stretched as he pulled himself up. He snapped his jaw at the air, revealing again the two long rows of venom-dripping teeth that worked on the skin of his prey like a saw. All he had to do was bite her once and wait.

The head rose, coming closer and closer to her foot. Snow and cold wind flew across his body. The reptile pulled back, about to snap, when . . .

WHUNK!

She brought the base of the lamp down against the side of his jaw. Koko seemed surprised, but not even annoyed. He snapped again, and again she swung, this time catching him on the side of the head, near his eye.

That, he didn't like at all. He bit, lightning quick, taking almost the whole base of the lamp into his mouth. His jaws had unhinged, making swallowing the whole thing easy. Chelsea choked, realizing the heavy base of the lamp was just about as wide as her shoulders. She could fit inside easily too.

Not wanting to lose her only weapon, she pulled, but the mouth, which could rip a horse apart, held on fast. Koko pulled back, just once, and she almost lost her grip. This part of the battle would only last a second more. She knew she was no match for his strength, having felt it, hard and heavy, through the metal feeding claw.

Unless . . . why fight it?

Rather than pull, she pushed, for all she was worth, driving the lamp deep down the lizard's throat. Koko made a pained huffing noise and yanked himself back off the statue. He snapped his head back and forth a few times, slamming the lampshade against the bed and the base of the statue, trying to loosen the thing in his throat.

For a few seconds, Chelsea hoped he might choke to death on the thing, suffocate right in front of her, but instead, he put his front legs on the pole and yanked. She could see the muscles of his throat working backward, pushing as his claws pulled. With a sickening rush, the base of the lamp popped out of his mouth, onto the floor, covered with thick mucous and a small chunk of cloth that looked like a piece of Dr. Gambinetti's Snoopy tie.

Then the lizard turned back to her.

That was it, then. She was done for. She briefly fought an urge to count all the tiles in the ceiling. Why not, really? What did it matter? *4, 5, 6, 7, 8.*

But no. She knew it wouldn't protect her, and if she had to die, at least it wouldn't be as a slave to that stupid disease.

A cold wind blew in from the broken window, across her face, down along Koko's back. He panted a few times, relieved to be free of the lamp. Then . . .

Maybe he'd decided she wasn't worth it, but more likely the cold from the window was getting to him. She remembered reading that Komodos only bred at a temperature of 130 degrees, so a Bilsford December must be a kick in the head.

For whatever reason, Koko backed off. For a second, it looked as though he might just leave the room, but on his way out, after what looked like some thought, he paused to pull Eve Mandisa's corpse out along with him.

As he yanked her through the hole in the door, she folded like a rag doll, her Mona Lisa smile and open eyes looking out at Chelsea before her head folded down into her chest and slipped through the gap, like a puppet bowing in an impossible puppet-way, saying good night and good-bye to its audience in a high-pitched cartoon voice.

After a few seconds, she heard Koko heading back down the stairs, maybe again planning to reach his basement nest.

1, 2, buckle my shoe.

Only this time, the heavy plodding and scraping of the dragon's tread was followed by the quieter thuds of Eve Mandisa's body as Koko dragged it along.

When Chelsea was absolutely certain that Koko and his former owner had reached the first floor, she tried to slide down from the heavy sculpture, quiet as a mouse. Briefly, she snagged the pocket of her blue jeans on the crocodile god's stone crown. The sudden cold pressure made her think of what Koko's snout might feel like against her, made her imagine what it would be like to have those sharp jaws clamp around her thigh and twist and tear, filling the wound with poison.

When she reached the floor she felt an urge to rub her hands in the little swirls of snow that rushed in from the broken window, as if washing them, and she didn't bother to fight it. Twelve times she rubbed, pretending the air from the winter storm was water, until her hands were numb from the cold and she realized that all she was doing, really, was wasting time.

She had to focus on what could really help her. Had to. And what was that? What could help her? What had helped her? The heavy lamp and the cold.

Where was the lamp, anyway? She looked down and saw it was useless. Aside from the fact it was covered in thick reddish gore that was probably soaked with venom, the lamp, full of teeth marks, had twisted free of its base. She could no longer use it to batter the window bars. Just as well. She didn't want to touch it anyway.

Slowly she crept over to the bed, pushed aside a suitcase, and sat down. Her heart was still beating fast, but not as fast as it had been, and her breathing had slowed. What should she do? What *could* she do? What was it Dr. Gambinetti had always said? Separate the fear from the reality.

So what was she afraid of?

That she was trapped in a house and a ten-foot Komodo dragon might come back up those stairs at any moment, attack, kill, and eat her.

What was the reality?

That she was trapped in a house and a ten-foot

Komodo dragon might come back up those stairs at any moment, attack, kill, and eat her.

Seemed funny. If her stomach wasn't hurting so much and her body wasn't shivering from the cold, she might laugh. Her teeth were chattering as she absently pulled at the blanket on the bed.

It occurred to her then that if it had been the cold that drove Koko away, maybe Chelsea could make things even colder. She wrapped herself in the heavy cover and then opened the remaining windows as wide as they'd go. Snow swirled inside the room in earnest now and when she exhaled into the wind, she could see her breath.

KUNK!

She turned toward the sudden sound, but realized it was the pipes clanking with heat. The old iron radiator was warm to the touch. Hadn't she seen a thermostat in the hall?

She walked up to the door, the one with the hole in it the size of a big lizard, and gently tugged it open so it wouldn't make too much noise. A few splinters of wood tumbled off and Chelsea noticed that the rough edge of the wound had a thick liquid on it that looked black in the dim light. Blood? Had Koko hurt himself climbing through?

Good.

It wasn't until she stepped out into the hall and looked down the stairs into the living-room lights that she remembered Derek was still down there somewhere. Or was he? Maybe he hadn't come to her rescue because he'd gotten out somehow. Maybe help would be coming any second. Or maybe he'd succumbed to the wound in his hand.

Count all the posts in the banister, or he'll be dead.

"Don't be stupid," she hissed under her breath. But as she walked along the second-floor hallway, opening all the windows wide, she counted the thin white slats on the painted paneling of the walls just the same.

There were three windows in the upstairs hall, now, all blowing snow inside.

CUNK!

She gasped and whirled in spite of herself. Just another steam-filled radiator, battling it out with the cold. To the right, though, on the wall above it, was the thermostat, looking oddly new in the midst of the old house. She walked up to the small plastic square with the digital readout. There was a switch on top with three settings—heat, off, and cool. She moved it to OFF then wondered about COOL. The house couldn't possibly have central air conditioning, could it? Eve Mandisa never could have afforded such a thing. Could the shut-in, trapped in here 24/7, have decided to make her prison more comfortable on hot summer days?

She flicked the switch to COOL and lowered the temperature down to zero degrees. Within seconds, she heard a steady rush of air from somewhere above. She stuck her hand up toward the sound. Though she couldn't see any vent on the high ceiling, a breeze hit her fingers. It could just be the wind, but she preferred to think it was air conditioning.

Eat cold, Komodo!

Excited now, she opened every door she could find on the second floor, opened every new window she came upon, inviting in as much of the stormy night as she could. As she worked, she scanned the two additional rooms she had found for anything she might use, but discovered mostly files and unopened boxes. There was another floor lamp, but it wasn't nearly as heavy as the one that'd saved her. There was also a dull pair of scissors and a metal yardstick. One closet was empty, except for an old curtain rod leaning against a bare wall.

She took it, and tossed it into a growing pile of pathetic, last-ditch "weapons." After all, maybe she could use one to poke out Koko's eyes. The image rose, only it wasn't a lizard's eye, it was hers, then Dr. Gambinetti's, then Derek's.

Stop it! Stop it! Stop it!

Only if you count.

She compromised, to keep her inner reptile at bay, recounting all the windows she'd opened. By the time she was done, Chelsea could hear the steam in the pipes gurgling back down, hear the wood creak as the house grew colder. The whole place would be freezing soon. Maybe Koko would go dormant or, better yet, maybe the damn thing would crawl into a corner and die.

She found herself a spot at the end of the hallway, where the stairs were still visible, sat down and wrapped the blanket tightly around her, as if she were sitting on a nest. The wind blew. Snow gathered in the dark. No way. No way would a cold-blooded lizard that needed heat and light want to come back up here. She felt proud of herself, if only for a few seconds.

Because her eyes were still glued to the stairs, watching, just to be sure.

Just in case Koko knew where the thermostat was.

KRUNK!

She lifted her head. That wasn't radiator pipes. The

156

heavier sound from below was followed by a thrashing noise and things falling. Koko was on the move. Chelsea craned her neck but saw no shadows from below.

What's he up to, then?

Cautiously she rose to her feet and stepped closer to the staircase. She'd left all the doors to the rooms open so she could run to any one of them and slam the door if he came back.

She heard the claws scraping against what sounded like hollow wood. The sound was steady but slow, as if Koko was tired. Was he at the kitchen door again? Why?

Of course. The cold was getting to him, making him more desperate for the only spot in the house he thought would still be warm: his nest. But that meant going through the kitchen. Crap. How could she be so stupid? What if Derek was still in there? What if he was unconscious?

Frantically, she pulled out her cell and hit his number on the speed dial. The battery was low, but after a few frightening seconds, punctuated by the sound of loud claws testing wood, he answered.

"Chelsea?" Derek said. His voice was really weak.

"Derek! Where are you?" she whispered into the phone, surprised at how hoarse her own voice sounded, how much it hurt to talk.

"Looks like the kitchen," he said.

"Are you okay? Are you still bleeding?"

"No. I mean, there's some blood, yeah, but it doesn't hurt anymore. I can still move some of my fingers. I think. Smells like hell in here with all the gas. Getting cold, too."

He sounded awful, maybe delusional. And the gas. He'd never turned it off!

"Derek, you've got to get out of there! Koko's at the door."

"I know. You think I can't hear him? L. C., I'm so tired. I think I'm going to fall asleep. It'll be okay. Something I gotta . . . something I gotta . . ."

It sounded like the door was about to give.

"No, Derek! No! Don't fall asleep! Please! I can distract him. I can throw something down the stairs. Can you get out of the kitchen? There's a closet in the hallway. Just get out of the kitchen, get into the closet. He'll just head downstairs to the basement. He needs the heat."

"But . . . won't he come . . . upstairs?"

Yes! Yes he will, and then you'll be his! He'll turn you into a lizard too, and you'll both eat Derek!

"No, he won't! It's too cold up here now. There's a

vase I can throw down the steps. When it lands, when he comes away from the door, you run into the closet, okay?"

"Hmmm . . . okay. I'm on my feet, kind of. I think."

Through the phone, she heard the door thudding, cracking.

Heedless of how much noise she was making, holding the cell phone between her teeth, she raced for one of the potted plants that lined the hall and brought it to the top of the steps.

"Ready?"

There was silence on the other end, except for the insistent banging.

"Derek!" she screamed.

"Huh? Yes! Ready!"

She put the cell back in her mouth, lifted the vase and hurled it down the steps. It cleared the last step and smashed against the floor by the front door, with a resounding, satisfying, wonderfully loud crash.

All at once, the sound at the door stopped. She could hear Koko turn his huge body away from the kitchen, clamber down the hall. The second she saw his shadow at the bottom of the stairs, she shouted into the cell phone.

"Now, Derek! Run into the closet, now!"

Koko's nose poked around the base of the stairs. He looked at the broken pile of dirt and pottery, then up the stairs.

All of a sudden, Chelsea realized he could see her. She backed away a step. Would he come up again? His tongue flicked out of his mouth. He looked as if he was deciding.

But then there was another sound, the creaking of the kitchen door opening, followed by a series of leaden steps. It was Derek, moving slow.

Koko turned back toward the sound. Chelsea hissed at him. He looked toward her, but slowly turned again toward the hallway.

The steps ceased. A door closed. Derek had made it! He was in the closet. He must be. But she had to make sure.

As Koko stared at her, she put the cell phone to her ear again.

"Derek?"

"Yeah . . . I'm in . . . It's . . . it's dark inside a closet. Kind of warmer, though. I think there's a bunch of coats."

"Try to wrap something around your hand," Chelsea said.

Koko twisted his head, watched Chelsea speak, then turned back to the hall.

"Derek, I think he's heading back to the kitchen now. Just try to stay quiet. If he doesn't know you're there, he'll just head downstairs."

"It's okay, L. C . . . . Don't worry . . ."

Koko's tail flicked out behind him as he vanished into the living room.

"Shhhh, Derek. Please, just be quiet."

He lowered his voice. "I just . . . want you to know . . . I reached your parents."

Chelsea felt her very soul exhale at his words.

"You did?"

Derek was panting. She wasn't sure he was trying to whisper. The low voice may be all he could manage. "Yeah . . . they're bringing . . . the whole cavalry . . ."

"I could kiss you!"

"You'd betterrrrr . . . crhhkkkkk." His words trailed off into a funny gurgling noise.

"Derek?"

She heard a light thud, as if the cell phone had fallen from his hand.

"Derek? Are you okay? Derek?"

She heard a strange noise, like a saw moving steadily back and forth. It could be the draft whistling in and out of the closet. It could be Derek trying to breathe.

It didn't matter, she told herself. He'd reached her parents. They would bring the police, the fire department, the army. They'd be saved. Derek would be fine. She only hoped he'd been able to tell them exactly how huge the lizard was, so they didn't come with small nets.

But then she heard another sound, loud and clear, both through the cell phone and from down below. It was a sound she'd heard too often tonight. Scratching.

Koko hadn't gone into the basement at all.

He was clawing at the closet.

It didn't make any sense. With the temperature down, Koko should be racing for warmth and security.

Without quite realizing what she was doing, Chelsea put her foot down on the first of the fourteen steps. Fearing for Derek, wanting to get to him, she even went down to the thirteenth. On the twelfth, she froze, realizing that every step she took made her more visible from the living room.

And what would she do anyway? Whistle for the lizard? Let Koko chase her back upstairs and hope help would arrive in time? She liked Derek an awful lot, more now than ever, but did she really, really and truly, want to risk being killed for him?

You'll be eaten, now and forever. You'll die, alone and terrified.

Even so, she couldn't leave Derek to Koko and live with herself—if she lived.

Oh, crap, here I go . . .

She put the cell phone in her pocket, then crouched down on the twelfth step. As it took her weight, it creaked, even more as she lowered her head and surveyed the view through the short slats.

It was probably a trick of fear and memory, but the living room looked different from when she'd fled it. What? Less than half an hour ago? It was almost like a theater set, deliberately arranged to tell its backstory, the setup for the scene to come. The lamp lay on the floor, its burning white bulb pressing against the crushed yellow shade, throwing a wide oval of light across the room and onto the tall windows half covered with frost. The couch had been shoved into a ruffled throw rug, probably when Chelsea and Derek fled for the door. The broken key was even still visible in the lock where she'd snapped it off. The heavy lounge chair Koko had crept up behind and knocked over when he attacked was rolled onto its side. Thankfully, it blocked her view of Dr. Gambinetti, leaving only his legs and feet sticking out.

As she stared sadly at his familiar brown corduroy pants, she thought she saw his black-shoed foot twitch, as if it were tapping in time to Koko's beating at the closet door. Could he still be alive, or was Koko just rattling the house?

She crept down a few more steps, the eleventh, the tenth, the ninth, until she could actually stick her head ever so slightly over the banister and peer toward the kitchen.

Koko was there, his thick, massive body wedged at an angle in the hallway, his back legs braced against the wall behind him, his front legs halfway up the closet door, scratching away. He looked like a big clay dog, trapped in a house built for midgets. A pile of wood scraps gathered at the floor beneath him, looking almost like the wood shavings in the rabbit pens at work.

Why was he there and not downstairs? Why did he want Derek so badly?

Koko's head bobbed back and forth as his claws worked. He looked as if he was either tired or engaged in some ritual lizard behavior. Chelsea took some small comfort in the fact that his efforts didn't seem as steady or ferocious as they had at the door to the bedroom, but really, she couldn't be sure. She scanned his body for a wound that might have left the blood upstairs, but saw nothing other than muscle and wobbly clay-gray flaps of empty stomach.

Maybe in all the excitement, he hadn't eaten enough.

On the floor below his hanging gut, though, mixed in with the closet door's detritus, there was a trail of wet, dark red splotches that led from the base of the closet door all the way back to the kitchen floor. If it wasn't Koko's blood, it was Derek's. His wound must be pretty bad. No wonder he'd passed out.

Maybe that was why Koko hadn't raced for the basement. The sight of blood meant another wounded victim was waiting. Or maybe his own brain had been fried by all the excitement, and he was choosing aggression over survival.

Chelsea wished she'd read more about the dragons, but the OCD had stopped her, as always. And now, today, in the real world, for all the OCD's claims about making her safe, if it made her hesitate again at the wrong moment, it might even kill her.

Not that she had a plan of her own, other than the stupid whistle and run idea. She took a final step down, to the eighth stair and just waited. Koko wasn't through the door yet. Maybe the police would get here before he broke through and Chelsea wouldn't have to do anything. At least now she could clearly see when the time was right. That would be the smart thing to do. If Koko breached the door she could scream. She probably *would* scream and Koko would come after her.

It was a decent plan, except for one small detail.

Koko turned and saw her.

They both froze, like ex-lovers embarrassed to run into each other at the same party. He focused on her face and they locked eyes.

His tongue flicked out twice, three times. Did he know? Did his reptile brain realize it was her fault the house had gotten so cold?

Leaning against the door like that, with his head at least five feet in the air, he looked almost human. But then his front legs slid off the door, one at a time, thudding on the hall's flower-patterned linoleum floor. Down on all fours he looked anything but human. He didn't look animal, either. He didn't look like anything that had any right to be alive. He looked like a dinosaur, a dragon, a primal force of nature. Something you had to make a statue to, or else.

His first steps toward her were slow, as if he were tired, or wounded, or freezing, or all of those. His head pivoted to remain fixed on her as he moved in inches. But then, without any pause, without any tensing of muscle, he darted across the floor toward the stairs with a sudden, startling burst of speed.

I've got to run! I've got to run now! Chelsea thought as she stared at the ten-foot blur. *Up the stairs! Into a room, any room!*

She would have made it too, had not the voice of the OCD rode the pulse of panic into her brain.

Count the tiles in the ceiling!

And, caught off guard, for a precious second, she obeyed.

2, 4, 6, 8.

She'd reached ten before she wrested control of her body back. By then Koko was at the base of the stairs and still moving fast. In seconds, he'd be upon her. She'd never make it up the stairs before he scrambled his 150 pounds on top of her 120, and brought her down. She'd be carrion.

She put both hands on the banister and leaped over it. By the time Koko had reached the spot where she'd stood, she was landing with a crash on the hallway floor.

Koko flung his body against the railing. It cracked and splintered. She looked up in time to see his snout and neck burst through as if the posts were toothpicks.

Now she ran. She ran full tilt down the hallway, nearly slipping on Derek's blood, into the kitchen where the air was thick with the heavy smell of gas. Not knowing where Koko was, not knowing how close he was behind her, she spun herself in the only direction available, toward the basement door. She threw it open. The moist, hot air from below slapped her in the face. She pulled her head back and then half fell, half ran down the stairs.

She looked around. Screaming her frustration into the moist air, she turned the dials for the heat and the humidity down to zero. The misting machine coughed once before falling silent. As she heard Koko coming down the stairs, she grabbed the only weapon available, the mechanical claw, and ran for her last hiding place, Koko's cage. Without really stopping to consider how Koko could have gotten out, she unbolted the door and dove in among the dirt and plants.

As the lizard curved itself around the base of the stairs, Chelsea reached through the wire above the Plexiglas and slid the bolt back into place, locking herself inside.

Koko ambled into the center of the ten-by-twelve area, taking up much of it. He raised his head and twisted it curiously, regarding her. It was almost as if he were admiring the irony: he outside in the human world, she stuck in there.

"Get out! Go away!" she screamed at him from behind the protective wall. She shook the claw at him threateningly. "I'll kill you!"

He hissed at her. *You and what army?*

He stepped forward, craning his neck into the glow from the three heat lamps. Great, now he'd be all warm and cozy.

Not if Chelsea had anything to say about it. Swinging the metal claw like a club, she smashed the heat lamp closest to her. There was a flash as a shower of glass hit his water dish.

Koko hissed.

"Didn't like that, eh? How about this then?"

She swung at the second. "Screw you, Koko! You hear me? Screw you!"

Koko hissed and reared at the second flash and breaking glass. When Chelsea smashed the third light, he slammed both front claws into the Plexiglas door. He stood there, propped up on his back legs, looking totally pissed in spite of his Kermit grin, as she destroyed the orange bulb.

Now the only lights in the basement were the

recessed fluorescents that covered the part of the room Koko was in. They made his gray skin look a little green. Chelsea was in semidarkness, panting, waiting, stretching her ears to see if there were sirens coming.

Where were they?

She stepped back and felt something hard under her foot. Looking down, she saw the frayed remains of the dog collar and remembered how Aristotle had snuck in. Maybe she could squeeze out? She looked up at the small window, at the piece of wood Derek had shoved there. The window she could manage, but what about the bars?

No. It was hopeless. She just wasn't as small as a little dog.

Where was Koko, anyway? She'd taken her eyes off him while she was looking at the window, and now he was nowhere to be seen. Had he gone back upstairs? Was he sitting in some shadow?

A quiet rustling made her turn to look behind her. The only thing there was the big nest made of sticks and straw and leaves that Koko traditionally sat on. She looked in horror as the whole nest shook.

It was only then she realized, eyes widening, exactly how Koko had gotten out. The big lizard hadn't been sitting on top of the habitat's dirt all that time, he was covering a hole he'd dug. There, out of sight, at some point, he scratched at the Plexiglas until he was able to slip into the small space between the Plexiglas and the cinderblock, and now could come and go as he pleased.

As the living hill rose, Chelsea scrambled across the dirt and twigs and headed for the locked door, each frantic move she made slowed by the moist earth and plants. Reaching her goal, she stood on tiptoes and jammed her arm through the wire, letting its sharp ends cut her skin as she reached for the bolt. She threw the door open with her weight and spilled out onto the floor.

At her back, she saw Koko following. She kicked the door shut, stood and slammed the bolt into place just as he hit the thick Plexiglas with all 150 pounds. The wall shook and creaked. White dust fell from the recessed ceiling. Koko stared at her a second as she raced for the stairs. A few steps up, she saw his tail again vanish under his nest.

As she reached the kitchen, she heard him on the steps. Now she knew just how sophisticated he was. An animal would back off, stay in the nest, but Koko, Koko was just pissed now and out for revenge. Worse, rejuvenated by what heat he'd enjoyed down there, he was moving faster. It was all she could do to barrel into the kitchen table, knocking it over and falling in the process.

As his great form swept into the kitchen, she dove behind the table for cover. Koko slammed into it, pushing it and Chelsea up against the locked rear door of the house, slamming her head against the wood. He clawed, bit and pushed against the Formica table top, trying to gain purchase on its slick surface. All he really had to do was grab the side of the table and pull. How long would it take for him to figure that out?

Sobbing, she surveyed the little triangle her world had become, how tiny it was, how limited, exactly as Dr. Gambinetti had warned if she kept listening to her OCD. It was just this little space now, shared with some of the junk on the table that had been spilled to the floor and been pushed here along with her. Some mail, paper clips, overturned salt and pepper shakers . . .

. . . and matches.

The air was cooler near the drafty door, the gas was not as thick as it had been in the rest of the room, but she still smelled it. All of a sudden, Derek's plan to blow his way out didn't seem so stupid. Maybe because now it was the *only* idea.

The table slammed her again as Koko pounded it. She scooped the matches up in her hand and tore one off.

As she did, the OCD screamed at her.

No, don't! You'll die! Count the scratches on the floor! Wash your hands until they're raw! Count all the dust motes in the house, but don't ever light that match! You'll die! You'll burn, and burning is the worst way, the worst way to go.

But then Koko's claws and Kermit head came over the top of the table and looked down at her in what she imagined was an expression of triumph. So she did it, she flicked the match in the book, saw the spark catch and burst into flame, saw the flame grow faster and hotter than she could have imagined.

As the growing white flame hit the rest of the matches, she tossed the whole book up and over Koko's head. He twisted his head up. For a moment she was afraid he was going to bite it and put it out, but he didn't. He just watched.

Maybe he was just a dumb, hungry lizard after all.

As the kitchen erupted in a blinding ball of white light, she figured that if she died, at least it would be better than listening to that damn voice in her head every day, at the very least, dying in this white heat would be faster and more merciful than even the jaws of the lizard.

At least Koko should be happy. It was warm again. Hot, really. Hot enough for a monster from hell.

Chelsea felt as if she were in the heart of a thunder-storm, not safe on the earth, but stuck between the two clouds that crashed into each other and crackled.

As the world turned to light, the force of Koko's powerful arms faded against the terrible wall of energy that swept toward them both. It slammed Koko and the table into her, lifted her and took them all into the door behind them. The metal table legs crumbled like wet spaghetti and the top kept coming, flattening her against the door, squeezing all the air out of her, but continuing to push.

Her eyes were closed, but even the insides of her eyelids were filled with white light and heat. She swore her skull and rib cage were crushed as the door came free behind her. She had no idea what had happened to her arms and legs. She only knew she was flying, falling, and landing in a horrible darkness.

And all that had taken less than a second.

When the motion settled and her consciousness caught up with the flow of events, she couldn't be sure, but she thought maybe she was on her back. She heard a rush and a crackling like fire, but her back and hands felt cold. In the blackness, she heard the OCD singing weakly in her head, sounding dazed itself:

I told you so, I told you so, and now you're dead. You're dead forever.

But she wasn't, and just to prove it, she opened her eyes.

At first everything was blurry. Far off, some reds and yellows swam together like fish floating in the air. The rest was grays and darkness, until a wave of heat hit her hard. It was a focused heat, and everything around it felt cold, as if little icy needles were jabbing at her skin. It reminded her of when she had had her ears pierced, only the feeling was slower and more insistent.

The thick smell of smoke brought back more of her senses. She coughed from a mouthful of the stuff, and then started breathing through her nose. The pain shooting through her ribs jolted her brain, made her focus.

The back of her head ached as she raised it. She could see now that the distant red and yellow were flames, licking like giant lizard's tongues at a gaping wound in the back of the house. In addition to the red and yellow, blue and white flames shot out from pipes where the stove used to be. The explosion hadn't just forced her and the table through the door, it had torn out half of the rear wall. And now the back of the house was burning.

She noticed the white of the stove about ten feet to her left, lopsided on the ground where it had landed. She and it were far from the house, maybe fifty feet. It was still snowing, she could see the individual flakes gently landing on the shattered bits of tabletop that covered her chest.

Finally, blissfully, she heard the sirens, not far off at all, getting louder.

But help was not the only thing coming this way. Something big and black and thick as a fallen tree trunk moved near the wreckage of the house.

Koko. Koko had survived the blast as well.

He was dazed, but he saw her lying there helpless, and was coming for her, following the final command his brain had given when fully conscious. One foot after the other, he came, hips and shoulders waddling like a giant push toy, his huge tail dragging behind him, making a thick line on the ground in the soot and the snow.

One step, two steps, three steps, more.

Chelsea tried to move, but her legs were pinned under the combined weight of the pieces of the table and the door. On her back, unable even to flip over, she dug her hands into the wet ground and tried to pull herself out by her fingers, but could not. Whatever strength had carried her this far was gone.

Five steps, six steps, seven and eight.

Her hands were filled with wet mud and snow, but her body did not move. He was coming. He was still coming, until all she could see was his big head with its unhingeable jaw, that and the flames dancing around it like a living frame.

He would always come for her. It didn't matter that the sirens were deafening now, that she heard the cars screeching to a halt. It didn't matter if the police came, or the army. Even if they took her a thousand miles away from here, this thing, this lizard would still be waiting.

Forever.

Inches away, Koko stood there, staring at her with his deathly ebon eyes. He flicked his tongue once, then stopped moving. It wasn't until the snowflakes started to land right in those black, unblinking eyes, it wasn't until they melted into little wet pools that ran down the sides of Koko's face, down into the crack that formed his Muppet grin, that Chelsea realized the dragon wasn't going to be moving anymore.

Two police officers ran up, guns drawn, circling Koko and her, keeping their distance.

"I think he's dead," she said hoarsely.

One of them nodded at something she didn't see, something that made them relax a bit. They both holstered their weapons and set to work pulling the boards off her. She was breathing again. It was hoarse and painful, her ribs ached, but she was breathing, and though the officers offered her their hands, she stood up pretty much by herself.

They spoke to her in reassuring tones as they walked her in a wide circle around Koko. As she passed the lizard's side, she noticed the huge gash in it, and the dark blood and entrails that oozed from it.

Not the cold, then. Not just the cold anyway.

The front of the house was a maze of flashing lights, the police, a fire truck, an ambulance.

"How many in there?" a red-faced paramedic shouted at her.

"Two," she answered, but it was still hard to speak, her voice rough from screaming. "Derek's in the hall closet, Dr. Gambinetti's on the living-room floor."

It was only after the paramedic turned away and ran off that she realized she hadn't mentioned Eve Mandisa.

Oh well, they'd probably find her anyway. No rush.

Out of nowhere she felt two arms grab and pull at her. It took her a few seconds to realize it was her mother, saying nothing, but hugging her so tightly her ribs hurt. Her father was there too, his arms wrapped around them both. In that big nest of family and winter coats, Chelsea let go and sobbed.

They stood there like that until a paramedic pried them apart so he could have a look at Chelsea. He sat her in the back of an ambulance, checked her cuts, her blood pressure, her heart rate. As he worked on her, Chelsea watched them pull two gurneys through the front door.

Strapped to the first was Derek, his head twisting left and right, his eyes moving wildly in his head. They steadied for a second as the gurney passed her, and Chelsea swore he grinned at her. If he could talk, he'd probably make some stupid joke.

"She seems fine, just some scratches and bruises. We'll need the ambulance for the other two, but you'll want to take her to County General just to check her out," the paramedic said to her family.

Chelsea slid out of the ambulance to make room for the second gurney. Dr. Gambinetti was still—very still—but his head wasn't covered with a sheet. Maybe he was alive too.

Seeing her standing, her mother hugged her again. Chelsea tried to swallow, to clear her throat, but couldn't. Gently, she pulled herself away from her mother's embrace.

"My throat's so dry. I really need some water," she said.

Helen Kaüer looked around and spotted the convenience store on the corner. "I'll get you some."

Chelsea shook her head. "No, it's okay. I'll go."

Her mother stared. "Don't be silly."

"I'm not. He said I was fine."

"I'll go with you."

Chelsea shook her head and pressed her palm against her mother's cheek. "I'll be fine."

There were tears in her mother's eyes. "You're not. You're not fine. You're going to the hospital."

"Okay. Whatever. Right after I get some water, okay?"

Without waiting for a response, Chelsea pulled away and started walking. Helen Kaüer tried to follow, but her husband gently held her back. He spoke softly, but Chelsea heard him.

"Let her go herself if she wants. We'll watch her from here."

She didn't need to hear the rest. The cacophony of fire hoses, shouts, and flames quieted a bit at her back as she made her way to the convenience store. Somewhere far off, she heard music and people laughing. Hobson Night was still in full swing. Most of the people in the town were enjoying themselves.

Snow gathered in her hair. Everything ached, but it felt good to be moving after having been pinned under the wood, felt good to be outside after having been stuck in the house. When she pushed the door open and walked into the cleaner air of the store, she noticed for the first time how much she smelled of sweat and soot. What a fright she must be to look at.

But right now she really didn't care.

"Dasani, please," she said, pushing a five-dollar bill toward the creepy man whose eyes were lines of folded skin.

They'd found Derek. They'd help him. Maybe even Dr. Gambinetti was still alive.

He put the change on the counter next to the bottle.

Only if you count all the change. Then they'll be alive.

She grabbed the coins and stuffed them in her pocket. The cashier stared at her.

"Aren't you going to count your change?"

In her mind's eye, amidst the frenetic, chipmunk chattering of the OCD, with all its horrid, comic-book images and insane, magical cures, she caught a glimpse of the stone plaque in "Restrooms" Gambinetti's unkempt, cozy little office:

WHAT MIGHT BE ALWAYS OWES ITS DEEPEST DEBT TO WHAT IS.

"No," Chelsea said, between gulps of water. "I trust you."

EPILOGUE

Anne leaned back against the cold metal frame of the cot behind her. The last remnants of the story faded, and she laid her head back against the ratty sheets to gaze at the ceiling.

"Crap," she whispered. *Still here.*

But it shouldn't have surprised her. She knew right off the bat that the story wouldn't be about her. No way. That Chelsea chick was mental, scared of everything. That was so not Anne—Shirley maybe, but not Anne.

She wondered how much time had passed since the bones had hit the winning combo. One of the problems with telling the story was that it consumed the mind so completely. She'd lost all track of time, and was totally oblivious to her surroundings. An hour may have passed. Two or three could have ticked away, and she wouldn't know it. Hell, a Komodo dragon, like the one in the story, could have come in, taken a bite out of her, and wandered off, and she wouldn't have even noticed, not until the story was done. That's why it was safer to play in a group.

Screw the group. There was no group. There was just Daphne, Mary, and Shirley. And then there was Anne.

Did she have time for another game? Another story? It would be dangerous. For all she knew, the Headmistress had finished tormenting the three girls and was wandering the halls searching for *her*.

She had promised the Headmistress she'd return to her room. She'd lied.

"Sue me," she whispered, then broke up laughing.

Two stories had been told this night already. Did she dare try for a third?

"Hells yeah," Anne said quietly.

She rolled her head and looked into the black nothing of the hole next to her. *This entire place is a big nothing*, she thought. *One massive hole in the world, filled with* nada.

Anne leaned forward and gathered up the bones. Just for the sake of ritual, she returned them to the

186

Clutch and pulled the strings to seal the vermillion bag. She counted to ten, thinking about the weird girl from the story. *Counting keeps the oogie boogies away,* she thought, amused. Then, she opened the Clutch and dumped the bones out into her hand.

"And what have you got there?" the Headmistress asked.

Anne's muscles tightened at the sound of the voice. She didn't turn to the woman. Instead she tightly closed her hand around the bones.

Then, ever so calmly, she dropped to the side and fell through the hole in the floor. She'd picked the infirmary for this very reason: its escape hatch. Though she could pass through wall and floor and ceiling, the bones could not. They were solid and if Anne simply vanished through the planks, they would be left behind, along with any hope she'd ever have of escaping this place.

So, she fell, clutching the bones. When she reached the dark pit of the basement, she glided to the cold stone floor. A monstrous boiler rose up in the shadows beside her. Crates and boxes, darker than the atmosphere, stretched out in this space like a small shadowy skyline. Rats squeaked and scampered as her form became solid among them.

Then she was running. She dashed through the corridors of boxes, carefully returning the bones to the vermillion Clutch as she tore around a corner. She found the door and threw it open. Behind her, she heard the great slapping steps of the Headmistress.

"Stop immediately," the woman called with her mind.

The sonic command hit the back of Anne's head like a board. She stumbled and then found her footing. At the stairs, she let herself fade to air, all except her hand, which still gripped the Clutch. She flew upward, back to the first floor. She soared through the infirmary and into the hallway beyond. Quickly she emerged into the great room with its tattered furniture and carpets of dust. Up the main stairs she flew, to the second floor. She considered returning to the classroom where last night's story had been told, but thought better of it. She needed to find someplace new to hide the bones, someplace the Headmistress (and those three other bitches) wouldn't look. The bones were hers now. *Hers!* She wasn't sharing them ever again.

Desperate, Anne tried to remember the layout of the orphanage. She knew it all so well, but her panic was making it hard to think. All of the classrooms were behind her. They took up most of the second and third floors. The dormitories were ahead. They would have to do.

A harsh wind blew at her back, announcing the approach of the Headmistress. Anne peered over her shoulder and saw her roiling black cloud form rise into the hallway above the stairs.

Anne fled down the gloomy corridor. She turned left and then quickly dashed to the right.

Daphne, Mary, and Shirley staggered toward her from the end of the hall. They looked dazed and lost until they saw her. Then all three girls snapped out of their delirium, eyes burning across the fifteen yards that separated Anne from them.

She didn't have time to deal with these three, but they were blocking her escape. The Headmistress would be on her in seconds.

Anne ran to the nearest door and threw it open. Once inside, she slammed it and began looking around for someplace to hide the Clutch. The room was lined with beds, like the infirmary, only without the metal frames. Here, the beds had wooden frames and tiny headboards. Many of the mattresses were slashed open. Others littered the floor. Unfortunately, the room had no nightstands. No chests of drawers.

Where should she put the Clutch? She didn't have much time. In fact, she had no time at all.

A dark mist was seeping through the door. Anne leaped back, flying through the room to the far wall. She put the hand holding the Clutch behind her back, searching for any last-minute hiding place for the bones. But even as she noted the hole in the window, the Headmistress appeared, looking impossibly large and furious. A moment later, the three girls were also in the room, and the sight of them scared Anne more.

They all looked totally freaky and pissed off. Daphne's face was twisted tight. Her auburn hair fell into her glaring eyes. Her mouth was cast downward in a stern frown. Next to her, Mary stood with her arms crossed over her chest. Her half-lidded stare was intense and hateful. But the worst one was Shirley. The Red Room had obviously cracked her majorly. She twisted a lock of hair until it tore out on her finger. She dropped this to the floor and started in on another strand. All the while she fixed Anne with dead eyes that seemed beyond pain or anger or remorse. She looked like a psychopath observing a helpless victim.

"Wretched whore!" the Headmistress roared. "Your

punishment will be merciless. Come with me."

"Oh no," Shirley said with a throaty growl. She took a shambling step forward and tore free another clump of hair. "She's ours."

TO BE CONTINUED

DON'T MISS

WICKED DEAD

Skin

"Want to hang after dinner?" Dan asked. "My brother's playing at the new coffeehouse over on Blackman Drive at eight."

Peter paused, feeling suddenly sorry. Then he shook his head. "Can't. Got a date."

"With a mirror?" Gerry asked wryly.

He thought about telling them, then realized he wasn't ready. He had to say something, though, and it shouldn't be a lie.

"No, with someone I met at the gym."

There, Dan wouldn't be mad if he knew Peter was with a girl. It was an unwritten rule.

"Where you hooking up?"

That detail seemed harmless enough to mention, so Peter's eyes lit wickedly as he answered, "Her idea. A cemetery."

When Peter finally arrived home, instead of recriminations, he was again greeted by the smell of cooking bacon. Furrowing his brow, he jogged into the kitchen and again saw his mother at the stove. His father was there too; as he set the table, he sang some ancient seventies folk song about his child turning ten just the other day.

If their clothing wasn't different, he might have thought they'd never left.

"Aren't you guys a little young for Alzheimer's?" he asked.

"You missed breakfast this morning," his mother explained. "And I wanted to scratch your reward off my to-do list."

Dad picked his head up. "Me, I figured rather than wait until something slow like cancer got me, I'd just have the heart attack in one day."

His mother shot a glance at her husband. "This will *not* be a regular occurrence. And you will *not* die without permission."

His father scrunched his face in mock disappointment. "Darn. I was so looking forward to the whole bypass thing."

She turned to the stove and pressed her spatula into the pan. A backward spray of grease rose above the rim as Peter came up, hugged her, and kissed her on the cheek.

"That's better," she said.

In five hours, Peter had gone from being horrified he'd murdered a man, to being in a new relationship with a girl he'd obsessed over for months, to this. If Frank hadn't given him up to the cops yet, he was probably safe there, too.

Even the drumming in the back of his head was gone.

"I am sorry about this morning," Peter said to both of them. "Really."

His father gave him a thumbs-up. "Good. I'd hate to think you felt it was appropriate to try to break your mother's wrist."

His mother sighed. "He didn't grab me that hard, Carl. I was just surprised."

But Peter felt a twinge of guilt. He knew she was lying.

His father, as he scooped some steaming eggs onto

the plate at his son's seat, allowed himself a parental moment. "Pete, you're very strong, and I'm proud of that, and we all get adrenaline rushes, but you, even more than most, have to be careful about snapping out like that."

"I know."

"With great power comes great responsibility. Like Spider-Man, right?"

"Right."

"Feeling better now?" his mother asked, bringing the bacon over to the table.

"Yeah. Fine. Great."

They looked at him, expectantly. "And?" his father added.

Peter didn't know what he was talking about. Did he want another apology?

"I'm sorry again? *Really* sorry?"

His mother shook her head. "He's just not a rocket scientist."

So did his dad. "Good thing he can draw. I hear that pays well."

After a few more beats, Peter felt incredibly stupid for not realizing at once what they wanted. "Oh. Right."

He stood up and pulled back his sleeve to show his tattoo.

At first his mother's eyes registered a kind of sad shock, as if someone had drawn graffiti on a painting she'd labored on her entire life. Peter was worried she might try to sue someone, but after she had a chance to take it in, her features softened and she just nodded.

"My turn," his dad said, spinning Peter around. Never one to linger on any artwork except Peter's, he smiled instantly. "Wow. How much did that puppy set you back?"

Peter told him. His father shook his head. Peter thought he was going to get a lecture on how to better spend his cash, but instead his father said, "You got your money's worth."

And then the cholesterol was passed around in steaming heaps and a splendid time was had by all. When "breakfast" was over, though, and he mounted the steps to get ready for the evening, he heard them drop the happy banter and talk in hushed, tense voices.

"See? He's in a much better mood. It must have been all the excitement and a bad night's sleep."

"Let's hope so. I just never thought we'd have to deal with anything like that at his age. He's never been violent before."

"Come on, Elise, you're paranoid. It's not like he's

building pipe bombs in the garage or anything."

"No. But did you see the look in his eyes? He was like an animal."

Violent. Animal. The words clung to him like a stubborn stain, even throughout his hot shower. They echoed in Peter's head as he stepped out and used a thick towel to pad the wetness off his tattoo, while letting the rest of his body drip-dry.

Violent. Animal.

No. He was just standing up for himself. Feeling his oats, his power in the world for the first time. He was feeling free from his parents, and from Mr. Gitman's expectations, and Frank—well, if anyone had it coming, it was Frank.

The guy was attacking him, after all. He was *lucky* he didn't get killed.

And his mother that morning. Well, that was a mistake, that's all. He would never hurt her, never.

The image of his hand snapping out like a cobra striking, clenching around her thin wrist, ready to crush it, flashed in his mind. With it, the shadow of the feeling returned, the sudden, incomprehensible feeling. He wondered, was he strong enough that if he hadn't managed to get control over himself, he would have broken her bones?

No, it was just a mistake. He was tired. Hungover from some drug.

Not himself.

He took the car keys, donned a light overshirt, promised he'd be back before midnight, and said good-bye to his parents, trusting their love, if not their smiles.

His father had offered the SUV, but Peter took the secondhand "station" car. Remembering Brianna's crack about a venti latte, he didn't want to emphasize any economic differences between them. More than once he'd heard her deride the overprivileged yuppies who were ruining the world. It was one of the things about her that tickled him. Her defiance. Her ranting against the machine.

Ah, he'd get her over to a Starbucks eventually, but he figured it would take time.

The older car, which smelled of worn vinyl and gasoline, started on the second try. As he pulled out and his neighborhood drifted off in the rearview mirror, he felt the secure side of his life, his home and school, let go of him, like fingers gently releasing his head from a comforting grasp.

He maneuvered the car past the shops and restaurants and into the southern half of Millerton, where rundown rental apartments further collapsed into empty lots, abandoned buildings, and finally Rizzo's tattoo parlor, and the little graveyard to its side. It was there, a few blocks from her aunt's home, where Brianna, after kissing him for the longest time, suggested they meet.

She sat waiting for him on a raised and cracked tomb beyond the remains of the wrought-iron fence, smoking a cigarette, still wearing the shawl and leotard. At that moment Peter realized he himself hadn't felt quite real since he'd left her. The rest of the day, filled with the banter of friends and family, now felt like some idle daydream, and this, this was the only thing that was real.

He wanted to run to her, but he managed a slow walk, maneuvering around the beer cans and empty crack vials that littered the final resting place of the dead. She saw him, he knew, but didn't look at him, choosing instead to stare up. Disappointed, he followed her gaze skyward to see what was so interesting.

Despite the glare from the streetlamps, more than a few stars were visible in the dark sky, poking between billowing white clouds like sunlight sparkling on the surface of a dark sea.

As he stepped closer, her eyes crinkled at the corners. She turned them to him, a warm smile spreading on her face. Her head was still turned up, though, and her shawl had fallen slightly back, its folds mixing with the shadows to create the illusion of wings. She looked like a faerie, a sprite. His own. For all his mother's warnings about appearances, nothing in his life had ever looked more perfect.

He paused for a moment to memorize the scene, planning to stay awake for days drawing it, over and over, until he got it just right. And then she spoke.

"You know, it's really weird to get the same tattoo as someone else."

"It's not the same," he said.

"You're right. It's not. It is nice, though. Like you."

He hopped up next to her on the stone slab and moved to kiss her. She put her hands on his chest, stopping him inches away from her.

"Don't you even want to talk to me?"

He made a face. She laughed. "You don't have to look so hurt! I just want to talk a little. I don't want to feel like you're, you know, just using me."

He smiled, remembering her earlier words. "You still think I don't know you at all?"

"Of course you don't," she said. "Not at all."

He imagined he looked hurt, like a puppy. "Then why'd you kiss me?"

She put a finger to his mouth and traced his lips with a long nail.

"Because when I saw that tat, I suddenly realized that *I* know *you*."

He disagreed—he *did* know her—but didn't want to fight about it, so he settled back. "Sure. Okay. I mean, yes, of course I want to talk to you."

It wasn't until he actually tried to think of something to talk about that Peter realized conversation hadn't been on his mind at all. He looked around at the broken tombstones, the litter, the overgrown grass and trees.

"So . . . why'd you pick this place?"

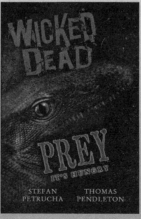